Sickly

Derrick Tillis

Author's Tranquility Press
ATLANTA, GEORGIA

Copyright © 2023 by Derrick Tillis

All rights reserved. No part of this publication may be reproduced, distributed, or transmitted in any form or by any means, including photocopying, recording, or other electronic or mechanical methods, without the prior written permission of the publisher, except in the case of brief quotations embodied in critical reviews and certain other noncommercial uses permitted by copyright law. For permission requests, write to the publisher, addressed "Attention: Permissions Coordinator," at the address below.

Derrick Tillis/Author's Tranquility Press
3900 N Commerce Dr. Suite 300 #1255
Atlanta, GA 30344, USA
www.authorstranquilitypress.com

Ordering Information:
Quantity sales. Special discounts are available on quantity purchases by corporations, associations, and others. For details, contact the "Special Sales Department" at the address above.

Sickly / Derrick Tillis
Paperback: 978-1-962859-36-3
eBook: 978-1-962859-37-0

Contents

Chapter 1 1
Chapter 2 10
Chapter 3 17
Chapter 4 24
Chapter 5 28
Chapter 6 38
Chapter 7 41
Chapter 8 45
Chapter 9 53
Chapter 10 68
Chapter 11 77

Chapter 1

"Todd," Derrick screams from across the street where Todd is standing. "What's up man, I haven't seen you in a while, went superstar and forgot about the people who protected you around these woods, "Hey, longtime man," Todd replies. "So how is Hollywood treating you, Todd? "Great," Todd replies with a smile on his face. "The old lady has been asking about you, she asks where's fire Marshall Bill?" Derrick says. "Man, I've been keeping busy with my dreams and wife, and you know, trying to grasp the whole signing autographs thing," replies Todd. "So, I hear your writing movies," said Todd. "Yeah! A little something, something. I wrote one called Goosebumps, but the title was already taken. You know when Halloween comes around, I can look forward to being sued for stealing my own idea," says Derrick. Todd and Derrick both start laughing. "How's that coming along?" asks Todd. "Not good, I don't have any money for promotions, biography, filming. Just another talented guy from Warburton Avenue with the same story as everybody else," said Derrick. "Look um, if you need me to pull a couple of strings feel free to ask," replies Todd. "You can do that?" Derrick asks. "Anything for my brother. Let's go see your mom, I'm sure she has a lot to scream at me about," Todd says. Todd and Derrick both start walking off towards Derricks house.

Door opens, "Hey! Pretty lady," Todd states. "Oh! My goodness, how are you? I watch your movies and tell my friends at work about you and Derrick growing up together! I still can't believe fire Marshall Bill is a superstar," says Lisa, Derrick's mom. "Well in this house, I'm just Todd mom" says Todd. "Well, this will always be home for you," replies Lisa.

Derrick returning from his room with five books in his hand and one that he started and needs to complete for his biography. "Todd," Derrick calls, "This is my masterpiece," Derrick says. "Looks like a lot of blank pages to me," states Todd. "Aw! Come on man, this is how Stephen King started," said Derrick. "Yeah! But Steven King had a nonstop, non-rejectful idea," both Derrick and Todd stated at the same time while laughing. "Well, you read this and tell me if you like it and I'll be sure to give you an autograph when I lay my hands down next to yours on Hollywood Boulevard," Derrick says while both of them smiling. "Hey, let's go to my house, I'm sure Corey would like to see you," states Todd. "Oh, you know Corey knows when we get together, bad things could happen. I got some cards and beers in the basement," replies Derrick. "C'mon with your crazy ass, get me into trouble ideas," Todd says. Derrick and Todd start walking across the street to Todd's house where Corey is with her best friend.

Todd pushes the door open, "Honey I'm home," says Derrick. "Todd is that you?" Replies Corey. "Naw, it's your friend and future godfather of your kids," Derrick replies.

—Sickly—

"Oh! My God, Derrick. how are you, we've missed you! This is Todd's best friend Derrick, from across the street. Derrick and Todd have many juvenile stories together," says Corey. "This is my friend Susan. Susan this is the one that set us up at school," says Corey. "Hello Mr. Popularity, I've heard so much about you," says Susan. "Did you hear that he still lives with his mom since he can't be alone," says Todd, laughing slightly. "Aw! Man! You just can't quit kicking me when I'm down," replies Derrick. "But anyway, I was thinking, when you think you can look over my script man? And give me a little insight of what you think," says Derrick. "Bring it by tomorrow and I'll think about it, if I think it's good, I'll pass it on to my mod-squad and bring you some good criticism," says Todd...

Meditation is the key to knowing who we truly are, like prayer, it's the thing that separates the need to need and the responsibility to understand. .aw shut up man, you're always talking about something nobody wants to hear, that boy wired wrong...All laughing as Todd briefly goes into a daze, he has a memory of when he was younger, a tragic moment in his life. "Todd" a voice whispers, "Todd." Todd slowly picking up his head to see what his brother wanted with him. "Yeah," replies Todd with curiosity and slight anger from being awakened. "Todd," Eric says again, eyes wide open and shaken, and urine along the floor at his feet. Todd looking down asks his brother, "What's wrong," pulling the covers back as if he were ready to leave his bedside. Todd had a feeling that there was something in the room but never spoke of it, his dad yelling in the background, "You guys better get to sleep or I'm coming in there." His brother says, "But Todd," starting to cry in whisper, "There's a monster under my bed." Todd, looking into his brothers' eyes as if he knew what he was speaking of a strange look as if he weren't alone. At this point, his brother shivering standing in the puddle of urine on the floor. "Okay" said Todd, "I'm gonna help you." His brother's eyes widening more, "Todd" he whispers, Todd looking down at his feet to see a hand slightly based upon the top of his brother's right foot, it looked creepy with long brown nails on its end. As Todd began to open his mouth to speak, Eric was swept under the bed, in an instant. The brother that Todd knew for the time he had lived was gone, shocked at what took place, Todd could do nothing but sit and stare off at the spot where his brother stood with one tear bearing from his eye, without a scream or any movement at all.

"Todd, what do you say, we go get our football on with some of the old men we grew up with in the hood," says Derrick. "Yeah, ah! Yeah, let's do that," Todd replied. Todd coming out of his daze, interrupted by Derrick. Confused and briefly surprised of a memory that he had seem to have forgotten about or blocked out.

The following night Todd sits back in his rocking chair going over the movie written by Derrick and what his character is based on. Its 10:30pm, Todd opens the book. He starts reading the script as if it were familiar like a book that spoke about him, a man of his own character. There's a noise in the background, Todd knowing his wife isn't home at this time pauses and turns his eyes slightly over his shoulder looking down that long hallway of his home, nothing, he turns

—Sickly—

his attention back to the script. He hears the noise again, curious, Todd stands up and walks toward the closet, not taking his eyes off the hallway, he slowly opens the closet door and grabs out a bat, slowly walking down the lighted hallway to his bedroom, there's a brief whisk behind him, as if someone is walking by moving fast. Todd stops and looks down, turns around with the bat in both hands, cautioned, paranoid, and scared, He slowly turns walking back towards the living room. The phone rings. Todd stops, taking a moment before picking up the phone on the fifth ring. Hey man, what you doing? I got a couple of six-packs, figured we'd have a drink or two or twelve and play catch up, before the misses get home," Derrick says. "Yeah, Yeah, that sounds good, come over, that'll be good!" replies Todd. Todd looking around with a feel of relief and smiling relieved by his kid friends call.

Later that evening Todd drives to the gas station to buy some snacks for his company arriving later that night. Todd calls Derrick and leaves a message on his phone, having overwhelming anxiety, looking around the gas station deli to find that there is no one present, not even the clerk. Todd walks from the freezer down the aisle, with curiosity, "Hello" says Todd, but there's no answer. The front door just closing for him to hear the chime of the bell on top. "Hello" Todd screams out softly, still no answer. Todd walks up to the checkout counter and looks around. He hears the voice of a woman whisper, "Todd." He smiles in disbelief, and says, "Okay, I'm convinced, I'm crazy," after dropping the jar of salsa on the floor. Todd reaches down to pick it up hearing the clerk ask him, "Sir, Do you need help?"

"Yeah, Yeah, sorry. How much will this cost me? You got a mop or something?" asks Todd. Clerk staring at Todd as if he's lost. Todd returns to his car and takes a breath. A voice is echoing in his head.

"Todd" ... "Todd" ... "You are more... Why run away? I need you to stop this, Todd. You are bringing badness to people…"

Later on, that evening Todd receives a call from Corey. "Todd, I received a strange call today from a woman claiming to be your Aunt Rose. She says she and your dad are sister and brother. I thought it strange, seems I haven't met everyone in the family," says Corey. "Yeah, you have, I just thought she would still be in the hospital and all, she's very sick. Remember I told you about the family members I lost when I was younger," said Todd. Corey replies, "Yeah, I remember, you said they all died or disappeared except for one and she went crazy."

"Yeah, well that's her. I tried to contact her for years, but she would not return my call or even write a letter," replies Todd. "Well, why now?" asks Corey. "I don't know," replied Todd. Todd staring out of the window, at his agents' office, into the dim, gray sky. As if something has come to him that he waited so long for, eyes wide, and face frowned. Brief silence as he puts the phone down.

That night Derrick comes over with Lisa before the game. "So, as we know, all bets are final cause my teams gonna kick some

—Sickly—

butt. And we aren't little boys no more so don't be crying and all that, everybody brace yourself," says Derrick. Lisa asks Corey, "So how's being married to a movie star?" "It's not the stardom I'm worried about, it's him. He's been acting strange lately, I can't put my finger on it, but I'm sure it's been ever since he received a call from his Aunt Rose," says Corey. Lisa replies, "Oh honey, don't worry about that, he has a lot of things in his past that he hasn't dealt with. His dad passing, his mom and her cancer. The thing that hurt him the most was probably his little brother, he had just disappeared one night, and no one knew how or why. Someone kidnapped him, he was never found, nobody reported nothing. So, for him to be doing as well as he is right now without any major fights or upsets, feel blessed honey. That man has a lot of pain. Hell, I'm surprised he's still sane himself. oh boy.

He loves you too, I see the way he looks at you. A man will love till it kills him, only if you love to pass the hurts." Todd briefly walks in the kitchen, where his wife and best friends' mom, Lisa, are watching him while cutting salad on a cutting board. "What are we whispering about or should I say gossiping about," asks Todd. "Nothing, just how much you're grown and how lucky you are to have me," said Corey, all three laughing out loud. "So how is Derrick getting along, mom?" asks Todd. "Well Derrick just broke up with his fiancé because she found someone that gave her the time she couldn't get from him, you know Derrick, always busy, full of ideas. That's why he's back home with me for a while. He feels sorry for me, his sisters and their husbands live out of state, but Derrick just wants what's best for everybody. He's very loyal to his duties as a policeman and protecting the young kids in the neighborhood, but he's happy in his own little way. And now that you've moved back, he's a bit more together you know," said Lisa.

Phone rings, "Derrick would you get that for me," asks Corey. "Sure, said Derrick. "Hi, it's Danielle, can I speak to Corey?"

"Sure, I'll get her right now, "Corey," Derrick screams into the kitchen not turning away from the television screen. "Yeah," Corey screams back. "The phone, it's your friend Danielle, by the way is she looking to be wedded, cause I know a fine young man that's trying to get swept off his feet and leave some insurance money with someone special..., besides his mom," Derrick joyfully replies.

Towards the end of the evening, with Derrick and Lisa heading out towards their home, across the street, the phone rings, Corey walking over to pick it up. "Hello", "yes", replies to the voice of an elderly woman. "How are you dear? May I please speak with Todd," the woman asks. "Sure, may I ask who's calling" replies Corey. "I'm Rose, his aunt, we spoke briefly before, and I was calling to tell him something very important. "Okay," replies Corey. "Todd," Corey yells softly. "Todd, it's that woman Rose again, your Aunt," says Corey. "Um!! Hello," Todd says. "Todd," asks Rose. Both Todd and Rose silent, not uttering a word, not replying to one another's uncomfortable greeting, as if spooked. Todd frowns looking off into the nothing of the outside as Rose finally began to speak... "Todd this is not a reunion, I have called you to warn you, there are some things you would like to know, some things I have answers to, and some things you may not understand. God forgive me. Look child, you are not at all,

—Sickly—

what you think you are, you are not haunted, you aren't plagued, you are not sick.

Everything that you know now is all part of the beginning, there may be an end, and there may not be for you. I'm so sorry child, I hated you and your brother, the two of you, along with your naive father who thought that he could ignore the facts, the reality of the facts," says Rose. "What are you telling me Aunt Rose," replies Todd. "I am not your aunt. I am someone who will help you only if you promise me something," says Rose. "Promise you what, I don't understand," says Todd. "In due time you will, in due time you will, goodnight child," says Rose. Rose, hanging the phone up, with Todd in suspense, wondering. "What is it honey? Does she want money? We should help her out, she's old and she's the only family you have now besides Derrick. And besides, the kids will need someone to tell them about their dad says Corey."

"What did you say?" asks Todd. "Nothing, I asked if you wanted to relax and watch a movie... So, are you gonna look into what's going on with your aunt? or,,,,,"

"Yeah! But I have a feeling she's not looking forward to a reunion, she sounds like she wants me erased," said Todd. "Erased? she didn't sound that way to me on the phone. What happened? asks Corey. "I don't understand." says Corey. Todd reaches over to turn the lamp off at his bedside after kissing his wife goodnight... I don't either. But I'm sure I'll find out. Don't forget to pick up the beer bottles in the morning and check the alarm for me babe. I really don't want to miss this says Corey.

Chapter 2

The following morning, Todd is awakened by the alarm clock screaming. He slams his hand down on top of it and slowly gets up looking over to see that his wife is not by his side. "Corey? Honey?" says Todd. Nothing, no response. Todd walks out into the hallway in the direction of the kitchen, "Honey," Todd calls out again. "I'm late Todd, I'm late. I told you I needed to get up early and you didn't set the alarm clock," says Corey. Todd looking at the bathroom door where the shower is running, "Honey, I'm sorry, I think I set it for 9:30 instead of 7:00 am," says Todd. "Don't be sorry Todd, be smart, you're always sorry, be smart. At least you're a good actor, sometimes you can fool yourself," says Corey. Todd bearing a look of surprise at his wife's reaction to his sincerity. "I'm going to throw out the garbage honey. I'll make some coffee when I come back," says Todd. Todd puts on his slippers and heads out the door to see the sky is gray, almost clueless to the dimmer blue shade of gray that he's never seen before, but no rain. Todd turns to go back up the stairs of his grassy yard, only to find that his wife's car isn't present at the time. Running back in the house, Todd yells to Corey, "Honey. Honey, your car was stolen. The bastards stole your car. They're probably joyriding as we speak."

—Sickly—

"It's not stolen, I let Lisa borrow it. Derrick had an arrest and could not pick her up this morning," replies Corey. Todd entered the bathroom, while his wife is in the bedroom at the time. He turns the water on and asks his wife to bring him a towel. "I can't believe you do not have the decency to clean up after the mess you made in this fucken kitchen with Derrick, Mr. Robocop, himself" says Corey. "Hun, relax, you're overacting and it's not even that time of the month, give me a break will you," says Todd. "I'll give you a break all right," replies Corey. "You okay in there," asks Todd. "Yes, I'm giving you a break," replies Corey. Todd hurrying to wipe the soap out of his eyes to attend to his wife, but before he finishes, she enters the bathroom very slowly closing the front door, with her back to the shower in her white robe and shoe less. "Honey, could you pass me a towel?" asks Todd again. Still no response, Todd whispers, "Honey?" Todds eyes burning from the soap, he opens the curtain only to find his wife staring at him, with eyes like the sun piercing with red bloodshot circles around her pupils and her teeth like a piranha, hair down to her shoulders and red, in her nightgown. Todd startled, slips in the shower bringing the curtain down on top of his head and his wife running out of the bathroom and Todd only catching a glimpse of her foot heel as she exits the bathroom running.

Todd quickly jumps up to grab the towel and slowly walks toward the bathroom door,

"Honey," he yells out, eyes wide open and piercing toward the entrance in fear. Todd walks out of the bathroom down the hallway toward his bedroom where the door creeks shut,

—DERRICK TILLIS—

"Honey," he yells out again, but no answer. Whisk, Todd spins around as the form of a woman walks pass behind him just entering another room, Todd turns around toward his living room. Ring, the telephone rings, Todd is slightly startled, but relieved. He picks the phone up off the wall and speaks softly, "Hello."

"Good morning honey. Sorry I didn't wake you up this morning. I left some breakfast in the microwave and took out the garbage. I should be home around 7:30 pm tonight," says Corey. Todd stands frozen, water on his body turns to sweat. "Honey? Hello? Todd are you there?" says Corey. Todd dropping the phone and turns around, as if he loses everything that means anything to him. His wife was not there at all, so who or what was accompanying him at this very moment. Todd says nothing and reaches for his keys and walks outside, backwards, with his back turned to the front of his home. "Ay! Man, you know you can go to jail for stuff like that right, you all out in the neighborhood spreading joy," says Derrick. "Derrick, I know this seems weird but I have a very good explanation that might not sound totally sane to you but your my best friend and I would appreciate it if you listened, please!!" says Todd. "What man, you okay, you look like you seen a ghost,' says Derrick. Todd not responding, Derrick stops smiling and looks at his friend knowing him for his truth. "Come over to my house and let's get you in some clothes man," says Derrick. Derrick looking over Todd's shoulder at the front door closing very slow without a breeze or any explanation at all, giving him Goosebumps.

—Sickly—

Later that evening, Todd and Derrick both sitting in Derrick's living room, Todd sitting in a rocking chair as if he were dazed off with sweat running down his face and Derrick asks, "Todd, you gotta talk to me. I've never seen you like this. You haven't eaten, you won't pick up the phone for Corey and you have that same look in your eyes you did when we were younger and i don't like it."

"You're my friend, I should be able to tell you anything. And on my life, I wish I knew how to tell you that either I'm crazy or everything that I've seen or felt or heard was true, but I don't know what's real anymore," replies Todd. "Todd what happened in that house that has you so spooked?" asks Derrick. "Do you believe in evil spirits? I mean feeling, seeing, hearing, everything. If you just say yes, even if for a second you believe I'm crazy and you laugh at me, but you still listen, I'll tell you everything," Todd says. "Yeah, I do, so tell me what's on your mind," Derricks says. As Todd tell Derrick the real story of his past and what just happened to him, his friend is open ears, not a blink. A concerned look shrouds his face, his sincere and ever awakened mind to his friend's pain and struggles with his past almost makes sense. The pieces of the puzzle that mystery about his friend all makes sense now.

Lisa enters the living room behind the chair that Todd is sitting in, she looks over at Derrick as if she was afraid, but she knew something and Derrick looks up at his mother, who looked worried and afraid and he asks, "Mom is everything okay?"

—DERRICK TILLIS—

"No, No, it isn't!! There are some things I would like to talk to the two of you about. Todd, you need to listen and be very open minded," Lisa said. "Trust me, I could not bring myself to open my mind any further unless I shot myself in the head," Todd says. "Todd, I knew your mother and your father for many years before you were born. There were some concerns when you and your brother were born, but your mother never let it stop her from loving you two, your dad on the other hand was a bit distraught, always drinking. Too himself, argumentative, until one day your mom sat down with me and explained why. Now honey I need you to listen to me and take what I'm about to say to answer the questions you've always had all your life without doubt or anger. Your mom and dad were unhappy because your dad couldn't have any children, they both tried for many years and then they just gave up. Well after they grew apart, your dad always accused your mom of cheating on him because she turned out pregnant. Well, your dad knew that baby that she was holding was not his own and your mom knew that too. But they also knew she hadn't cheated or even thought about such a thing, she loved that man, but your dad couldn't bring himself around to loving you. So, on your 1st birthday, he decided he would get an operation to help with the problem he had and that indeed made a difference. One year after that, she got pregnant again with your brother, your father was proud. But she didn't make it home and that brought him back to the beginning, back to drinking and carrying on. He raised two sons alone, and one of them wasn't his own, and when your

—Sickly—

brother disappeared, your father gave up. You were left alone. Your mother could not tell me who your father was, she just said, there's always a place for you in heaven cause you're special. And with that being said, I never asked or inquired. All I knew is that you were a good kid, and the answer will come to you one day, and I prayed for you every night. And I will continue to do so," explained Lisa.

"Thank you, Lisa, I just wish my god was as good as yours and I believed as much as you do, but I would be lying if I said I did, but I love you. Ma'am, you're the only mother I've grown to know, and again I thank you, I just have a feeling this won't get any better. I've had so much good in my life, but I forgot who I was as if I deserve it. But now my life has found a way to remind me, and I have some things I need to clear up," says Todd. "Well, I guess we need be asking your old aunt Rose some questions, what do you say bro," says Derrick. "Your right, she is my father's sister, I understand why she treated me like an outcast now. Hey! I need to call Corey, she's probably worried," replies Todd.

Todd picking up the phone to call Corey. Serious and confused but still almost content with a feeling of urgency to find the aunt whom he hasn't seen in over a decade. Phone ringing in Corey's coat pocket. Phone rings three times with no answer, until voicemail picks up. Todd leaves a message, very brief, "Hun, give me a call when you get this message okay."

A couple of hours pass, before Todd receives a return call from Corey. "Hey, Hun, sorry I couldn't get to you right away,

—DERRICK TILLIS—

I was very busy with a client. But I miss you, I was thinking maybe when I get home, we could have a little you and me time without being recognized or posing for pictures right here at home. I thought I might give you a chance to show me how much a movie star is really worth (laughing), if you know what I mean,' says Corey. "Yeah, honey that sounds good. Hey, listen I have an idea, why don't we take a trip to Westchester County and visit my aunt this weekend. I haven't seen her for a while and I have something I need to discuss with her," says Todd. "That sounds great!! I'm all for it. See you when I get home," replies Corey. "Sure, bye now," says Todd.

"So how about a road trip? Gals and guys. Trees, green pasture, and mountains how does that sound?" asks Todd. "Hell, yeah!! I need to get away from all this hot land and pollution," replies Derrick.

Chapter 3

The day is graceful, noon hours, bright sun, the trees green and there's a feel of relief for the four.

"So, whose great idea was this anyway and why didn't I come up with it," says Susan. Everyone laughs. "Well, it was Todd's! He has some family business to take care of and insisted we both bring our best friends along," says Corey. "Yep, cause we all know you gone need me, you know, when things get a 'lil crazy," Derrick says while everyone laughs. "See laughter is good for the heart," says Derrick. "Look! Look!

Honey look over there, see the hawks, I used to come out here when I was a kid and watch them swoop down on all types of small animals, it was amazing. What I wouldn't do to live out here. Derrick didn't we always say that when we were younger?" Todd says. "Yeah man, but then we grew up, you know. But I think it'll be a nice place for you and Corey to live and have kids, the whole married thing, you know," Derrick replies.

They pull up to an old mansion that overlooks the palisades and the Hudson River. Exiting the car Todd looks as if the location was not the same but the mansion looked familiar, looking at his map a third time he shakes his head with disbelief.

—DERRICK TILLIS—

"Todd, are you sure we're in the right place? Because I don't remember this at all being where your aunt lived. Nor do I remember her being all together so whatever you have on your mind bro, trust me, I am not at all about smiles," Derrick says. "Your right, so I'm sure you'll be the first to know exactly what I'm thinking," Todd replies. "That sounds more like it" Derrick says.

Corey and Susan astonished by the views. They have no idea what the whispers are about, nor do they have the slightest idea as to why they are even there. To them it's just a vacation. Todd and Derrick approach the front door without grabbing Todd rings the doorbell.

"Hello! Hello!" A gentleman's voice is heard through the door. "Just a moment," the gentleman says. A younger gentleman between his 20's and 30's opens the door and says, "Well hello!! *Mi casa es su casa*. How or why am I being blessed with company or help for that matter?" He asks.

"Aw, I'm sorry! I think I have the wrong house," Todd says. "We definitely don't have the wrong house but…Before Derrick could finish, the strange gentleman states, "Before we go any further, I know who you are. I don't know why you're here. All that stuff upstairs in the attic shouldn't mean anything to you now. I watch you on the big screen (smiling). Hey, I'm sorry I didn't introduce myself, my name is Jason, I grew up in this house. You don't remember me, but I remember you, just not the two beautiful ladies that are accompanying you. So how may I be of service?" Jason asks.

—Sickly—

"Well, I would like to know where our rooms are and a steak well done with a nice big bottle of champagne," Derrick says while smiling at the fiend with curiosity. "Hey is there a store nearby or a gas station, or something," Todd asks. "Well, you're in luck, we don't have red meat, sorry, but we don't have anything other than champagne, so if you want water we have tap, nice & cold, pure leaded and chicken in the freezer," Jason says. "Susan let's go upstairs to our rooms," Corey says. "Any room you find is yours. So, Todd, can I have your autograph before you leave? I would really appreciate it knowing I was sharing the same roof with a star," Jason says. "Sure, that wouldn't be a problem. So, who do I make this out to? You or a girlfriend?" Todd asks. "Your name would be just fine," Jason replies.

Later on, that evening, everyone sits in the living room around a small fireplace discussing the origins of the ancient house and its infrastructure. "Boom" There's a loud knocking upstairs that draws everyone's attention.

"Aw, don't pay that no mind, the mansion is settling. I used to think the house was alive at one time," Jason says while smiling. Derrick looking very serious as if there's something else going on. He looks over at Todd awaiting confirmation for his suspicion. Todd ignores it knowing that Derrick has never steered him wrong.

"Hey Derrick, you feel like walking me to the little ladies' room and waiting outside?" Susan asks. "Yeah, no problem," Derrick replies. Derrick not smiling, as if all his humor turned into suspicion. "Hey, there's a closet full of towels and feminine effects just in case you need. If you need help around the house or have any questions, just knock on my door, I'll be up, I don't sleep much. So, you guys have a good evening," Jason says. "Honey, this house is spooky in a sneaky, sexy kind of way. I wonder how long he's been here. Where would you go for entertainment around here?" Corey says.

Derrick and Susan walk upstairs to the mansion halls. Depicted pictures of older generations are all throughout the halls. "I know when I feel something and right now, I feel something, so how you feel Susan?" Derrick asks. "Hmm!! "I'm glad you asked, cause if were both feeling something we should express what that something is," Susan replies. "Don't get me wrong, I'm attracted to you and maybe we'll get married someday but right now, I don't like this feeling I'm getting about this house," Derrick replies. "Now that you mention it, I feel like we're being watched. You know what, never mind, I'll wait to use the bathroom, there should be one downstairs anyway," Susan says. "Shh, shh, shh!! I hear something," Derrick says. Derrick gazing down the long corridors of the hallway in suspense. He looks deep into the dark as if he's waiting to be greeted by someone or something. "Okay!! It's time to go back, but before we do, I want you to ask yourself why a hallway with no windows and a dim light would cast a shadow on a wall where no one is standing?" Derrick asks. "I think we should head back downstairs now," Susan says. While gripping Derrick's arm she says, "Derrick c'mon." Derrick turns slowly to follow Susan, while still starring down the long hallway at the shadow. A brief silence and pause, almost handicapped, Derrick's

—Sickly—

legs will not budge. He stares at the walls of the windowless hall and says very quietly, "We got to get out of here; I've seen enough movies to know when I'm in the wrong place."

"Hey Derrick, you two okay up there?" Todd asks. "Honey, you think Jason can show us where the puzzle garden in the back leads to tomorrow? This place is very interesting," Corey says.

"Todd, we got to get out of here man! There's no time to explain, we'll talk on the way to the car and outside the gates," Derrick says. "What's wrong? What happened?" Todd asks. "I just said we'll talk outside the gate," Derrick replies. "Look I'm going, Corey we need to leave, there's some weird shit going on here," Susan says. "JASON," Todd yells, but there's no answer. "JASON," Todd yells again, still no answer. "Okay I'm convinced. Listen Derrick maybe since we're on the same page now, you'll believe me when I tell you something I've never told anyone before in my life," Todd says. "Okay, you are all scaring me, the jokes over," Corey says. "Oh, this is far from a joke, you know I can be a comedian at times but Corey, honey this isn't the time. Give me your bag and forget the hospitality, we need to leave, NOW!!" Derrick says.

Derrick grabbing Corey's and Susan's bag, while Todd looks on toward the stairway, confused. Not one thing in the ten hours they've been present in the mansion. While exiting Todd says, "I feel like we've done all this traveling to run into a rock with a personality that wants me dead, for what, I don't know." Todd laughed angrily, while sitting in the passenger seat. Corey and Susan in the back seat both scared, and unsure of what had just taken place and why.

—DERRICK TILLIS—

"Todd, is there something I need to know? Is there something you know?" Corey asks. Corey awaiting an answer while being ignored by Todd. "I saw a hotel in the next town. Damn all this driving and none of us thought to stop for gas," Derrick says. "Pull over," Todd says. "What," Derrick replies. "Pull over," Todd says again. "You picked a good time to want to pull over. I wish Ashton would come jumping out of the bushes with a camera, but how would he explain the hair standing on the back of my neck when it's supposed to be a joke," Derrick says.

"Derrick, do you remember Eric? Because the only thing I remember is him looking at me in the face when he was taken from me and my dad. I remember when he disappeared how my dad went into this deep depression, drinking and trying to remember something he wasn't guilty of. Do you know my dad told the cops three years later that he murdered my brother? Never once did he ask me what really happened, I never once mentioned it to him. He barely said a word to me after my brother died. You know I never seem to know what's going on anymore. I'm seeing things, I'm hearing things. I laugh because at times I think it's funny that I might be going crazy, maybe you are to," Todd says.

"Look man, for a second, I thought you might be a little topsy turdy, but then again that's just you. But lately things have been weird; I mean the kind of weird where I'm even convinced. I don't know if you noticed, but when we were back there I that creepy hotel me and Susan, well Susan can speak for herself can't you?" Derrick says.

—Sickly—

"Susan what, look just take me home. I'm sorry to ruin your weekend, but the things I saw you only see in movies, and I don't see any cameras around," Susan says.

"Okay, what's going on? You're talking about weird things in the halls. Todd talking in his sleep and Derrick you're a real good friend to agree with him and all his stories right now. None of this makes any sense. Can we just get back in the car and go home, we all need some sleep, and I don't care for this red riding hood surrounding much," Corey says.

"Hey, how about it? Why don't we all just pretend that nothing's going on and go back home and forget the whole thing," Derrick says. "Exactly," Corey agrees. "No, not exactly Corey, we need to see what's going on with us before whatever is creeping us out makes its way to whoever or whichever one or all of us it's after," Derrick says. "I'm not worried, I'm more curious as to why," Todd says. "Can we just leave now, I don't want to be here anymore," Susan asks.

"We'll do that, hey Derrick? Do you really believe that something is out there or is this all a paranoid run for nothing? I mean it is funny, wow!!" Todd says while laughing. "Todd let's go home; I think you need to speak to my mom. It's a lot that you should know that I can't tell you because I didn't believe it, but now I'm starting to think that all this shit makes a hell of a lot of sense. Yeah, I said it, shit! Don't be surprised because I have a feeling, we're about to be knee deep in it," Derrick says.

Chapter 4

"Mom!!" Derrick yelling from outside while walking toward the house, "Mom," he yells again. "What boy? You are disturbing my studies with all that yelling," says Lisa. "Mom, we came back early, great trip," Derrick sarcastically gestures to his mom, while all but Susan is walking in the door. "Well, what happen?" Lisa asks. "Not much of anything out of the ordinary," says Derrick. "Todd," says Derrick softly, "You wanna brief her, or should I?" asks Derrick. "No, I think I'll tell her what's been bothering me," replies Todd.

"Lisa, I do have a question before I start sounding crazy," says Todd. "I'm sure i can help you with most of the answers, but I can't answer the question that you're afraid to ask because I don't know that answer. And to tell you the truth, I'm afraid to know who does," replies Lisa. Todd smiles with disbelief while sweat is starting to drip off his chin. "Afraid. There is something totally wrong with this picture. I mean I feel strange, I see things, I'm hearing voices for Christ's sake and I'm being mentally and physically abused for some reason. I mean there are no cameras around, I'm still waiting for the director to say cut. If you know anything, I mean anything Lisa, I'm begging you. Please, tell me," says Todd. "Okay!! The truth is your brother was never found the night he disappeared and only you and him were in that room that

—Sickly—

night, Todd. You know what you saw if you saw anything," says Lisa. "I'm gonna run upstairs and empty out my bags," says Derrick. "Stay right there. You are one of a kind Todd, and when the time comes, when the day comes, you need to remember and not be afraid to speak, you can't keep running. You know you're not crazy. We all know you, Todd. But do you know who you are? Do you know what your purpose is? You have money, you have fame, you have love," Lisa says with a lump in her throat. "We are all your family. Now child, what I think is not what I would have you believe, so in order to clear some things up and you get a bit closer to the answers you need, I have one request," says Lisa. "Anything," replies Todd. "Sunday. I want you to come with me to church, I know you don't believe, but I'm sure you'll find more answers there than anywhere else right now. And you know I'd never force you or fool you. But there's someone I want you to meet, and maybe you'll get your answers and I'll be right there holding your hand. Is that okay?" asks Lisa. "Sure," Todd replies with an uncertain look.

On the way-out Derrick sees Todd at the door with Corey standing by at the gate. "Listen bro, if you need anything just open the window or use the flashlight, I'll be up. And Todd, make sure you get your ass to church with moms on Sunday," says Derrick. "I will, Derrick! I always knew I had family across the street. Tell mom I said thank you," says Todd. Derrick slightly teary-eyed replies to Todd, "no doubt, now get some rest, we have a big day tomorrow."

—DERRICK TILLIS—

Day turning to night, Todd sitting in his chair in a daze. With much on his mind, Corey watching television beside him. Derrick laying down on the couch at his home with an ease to him, some candles lit with a book in hand, lights dim, relaxed. Derrick reading to himself slightly smiling. "Boom" a loud noise in the background. Derrick jumps up with a curious look on his face. "Mom, is everything okay?" Derrick asks. "Derrick what's with all that racket I'm trying to sleep," says Lisa. "Mom did you hear that?" asks Derrick. "Hear what Derrick? Please now I'm trying to sleep," says Lisa. "Okay, mom! Sorry, false alarm, I love you, good night!" says Derrick. Derrick looking around while talking his mom back to sleep.

Turns his attention toward the window, walking slowly, in the far view outside the window, just a way across the street. Derrick sees Todd staring in the window, as if he were looking right into Derricks eyes. Derrick waves his hand to say hello. Todd giving no response back, Derrick backs away from the window slowly reaching for the phone. "C'mon Corey pick up, pick up the phone," Derrick says. "Hello!" says Corey. "Corey! What's Todd doing right now?" asks Derrick. "Todd's asleep! Why? What's going on?" Corey asks. "Where is he asleep at, wait, wait, wait, is he asleep in the living room?" asks Derrick. "Yeah, in his chair, why? Is there something wrong Derrick?" Corey asks. "Corey listen to me, listen closely, don't ask any questions, just trust me!" Derrick says. "Oo, Okay!" Corey replies. "Corey walks over to Todd and looks in his face and tell me if he's okay. From here he doesn't look too good. Corey walking over to where both, she and Todd

—Sickly—

can be seen from across the street. "He looks okay to me, he's just asleep," says Corey. "Corey wave your hands in front of his eyes," says Derrick. "Why? He's asleep, his eyes are closed," says Corey. Derrick drops the phone knowing that there is something wrong with his friend. Not curious anymore, all his questions have answers now, the hairs raise on his arms and a brief rush runs through him.

Derrick looking on at his friend, knowing he has yet to blink, and he has no explanation for what's taking place right now, he runs toward the door. Corey still saying his name on the other end of the phone. "Thump, thump, thump," there's a knock at the door. "Who could that be this late at night?" Corey says. Corey opening the door. "Hey Corey," says Derrick. Derrick walking pass Corey into the house only to find Todd sound asleep in his chair. Derrick looks at Corey and back at Todd with confusion, he smiles. "You know what? I need some sleep. I woke my mom up, I'm about to wake Todd up, no more coffee for me, sorry! Listen when he wakes up, tell him if I'm not awake in time, do not wake me," Derrick says. Derrick smiling and walking back towards the front door. "Derrick you should really get some rest," says Corey. "Yep, I'll do that, good night, Corey! See you tomorrow," says Derrick. Derrick slowly walking towards his home and Corey slowly closing the door.

Chapter 5

The following morning, the sky is grey, the day is rainy, and Todd's alarm goes off. "Honey wake up, you gotta go, Lisa's waiting," says Corey. "I'm up, I'm up!! I need some coffee," Todd says. Todd rubbing his eyes looking at the window with the rain bouncing off of it like sleet off the windshield of a car. Telephone rings four times before Todd answers, "Hello?"

"Hey you up bro?" Derrick asks. "Yeah, yeah, I'm up.

I'm gonna hit the shower and give you a call back," replies Todd. Todd turns the shower on before hearing the phone ring again. Todd looks back and grabs the phone before the fifth ring with, "Hey you up bro?" Once again Derrick asks, Todd replies with, "Hey I told you I'm up, let me get in the shower before Lisa kills me c'mon." Derrick's voice repeating itself on the phone, "Hey you up bro?" Todd stops smiling and hangs the phone up with a slight frown on his face, not thinking about what just took place, he steps into the shower.

"I hope I can use my rain check this morning, you know how I like rainy days and how hectic it could be for me at work. I'm just no good without some type of stimulation," Corey says while smiling. "Honey! You know I would love to keep you here all to myself, but I have to go with Lisa, I promised," replies Todd. "Aww, okay. But do you promise to

—Sickly—

make it up to me later along with a foot massage and some chocolate ice cream," asks Corey. Both laughing while holding each other and rocking back and forth under the steamy water. Todd says, "Honey, I'll pull the moon closer and push the clouds away for you." Corey replies, "Not fair honey, I saw that in a movie cheater, try harder." Bother Corey and Todd smiling at each other while Todd steps out of the shower to grab his towel.

The doorbell rings, "Just a minute," Lisa yells down the stairs. "Ma, you and Todd go ahead I'm gonna be running a little late! Hopefully I'm not punished for it," Derrick says. "Well good morning, Todd! It's great that you made it, I always knew you would. Now remember, if you feel at anyway uncomfortable in the lords' house, then by all means, you leave freely, and I'll kindly follow behind you. Okay?" Lisa states. "Naw, I think I'll be fine, people are just a bit different from cameras that's all," Todd says while smiling. Both Lisa and Todd leaving to church. Todd with a look of curiosity on his face, but in his eyes there's a distant, almost afraid look.

Nearing the church where the pastor is greeting all of his visitors, newcomers, and residents. "And how are we today Ms. Lisa? Always a pleasure," pastor Nicholes says. "How are you today sir? I brought along a friend, his name is Todd," says Lisa. "Todd, and every day is a blessed day when there's new faces to visit us and become a part of our family. I'll be sure to send a special blessing up to bring you back after this visit," Pastor Nicholes says. "I'm happy to be here today sir," replies Todd. "We'll see you inside pastor," Lisa replies. "Yes, you will," says pastor Nicholes.

After a brief congregating on the outside of the church, everyone is ready to be seated with the pastor standing ever so ready on the podium with all his followers at attention to receive the lord's word. But unease sets in with Todd, adapting to his environment he relaxes himself.

"Before I start my pointing fingers, I would like to confess that I have negative feelings today about a lot of things that have been not heard but seen in the eyes of the lord. The eyes of the beholder, our father has revealed to me some news that he, can only change, now is there anyone in this house right now that would like to share something, anything. If you do not wish to speak now, you may take it up with myself and God, erase it and never let it show its ugly face again," said Pastor Nicholes.

"I have something to share pastor," says the blind man. "What would that be brother? Feel free to share what's on your heart," says the pastor. "Father, I don't know if you'll believe this one, but I can see," says the blind man. "And what is it you see my brother?" asks the pastor. "Father if I pointed at what I see today, what will take place in this house?" asks the blind man. "Well as always and forever we will give it up to our father and wait a second for it to come back down," replies the pastor. The blind man standing up with the help of his daughter next to him. Turning toward the seated area of benches where Todd and Lisa are. He raises his hand, pointing his finger in the direction of a hand full of people

—Sickly—

and turning very slow until he comes to a complete stop at Todd. Todd smiling very uncomfortably almost starting to sweat. "I see a man, I see a man. Could I tell you what he looks like father?" asks the blind man. "Tell us brother, in this house we all look the same to god! So, tell us," replies the pastor. "He looks like something I only ever dreamed about but never spoke about. He has red hair father, he has tire in his eyes father, black wings on his back father," says the blind man. Todd sweating and staring at the blind man in fear, the pastor looking on with suspense, the house looking at the man knowing him to be blind but at sight, this is what he sees. "He has power father. And you do not belong here. How did you get here, inside this house of god and pretend?" asks the blind man.

"Now look, were all here to find the lord and some of us have, but there's always a first time for everything," says Lisa. "Stop," the pastor yells out a cry and by his side he found himself alone and he doubted our father. "He rose from the grave for us only to be pained again by the sins of our people. We need not judge a newcomer here but embrace him with open arms like our father will us, if we believe in him," said the pastor. "You are not meant to be here; I can see you!" the old blind man whispers to Todd softly from across the church. "I'm sorry! I think I'll be on my way, this is not for me, I'm sorry Lisa, I apologize I gotta go," said Todd.

The people of the church looking on in awe. As Todd walks towards the doors of the church to exit, the pastor removing his glasses slowly from his face with a frown, he knows something about Todd isn't right. Lisa stands up to watch Todd rejected by her offer to live with him. He hurries so she may not follow him. Todd starts running down the street frantic. With the rain in his face, crossing the street with no safe thought about oncoming traffic, into the fog until he can't be seen no more. Todd frantically runs until he is out of breath, until he can no longer see his hands, until he can no longer see what's in front of him.

He stops only to find that he is not alone. Todd looks around in panic while saying, "Hello, Hello!" A voice whispers, "Todd." Todd hears his name called by a very deep voice that shakes him, wide eyed he turns around in circles. "Is somebody there? Hello, is anybody out there?" Todd asks. There's a dark profile in the distance of a man. As Todd gets closer, he gets angry, speeding up, only to find that he is still alone. There is a vague glimpse of a horse in the distance, the rain starts to change into sleet, the fog starts to clear. On his waist where his phone would have no reception, it blinks to tell him there are missed calls and messages. To Todd that moment was as long as twenty minutes, for his friends and family, in search of him, it was twelve hours that had passed. Todd would find himself not wanting to speak for the next couple of days.

The doorbell rings at Todd's home. "Who is it?" asks Corey. "It's Derrick, Corey, I came to check up on Todd, see how he's doing," says Derrick. 'He hasn't said a word since he's come back. I don't know what to do anymore, I didn't want to call his doctor because he might think that he's crazy. He's been jibbering something all night," says Corey. "Corey! I think we need to talk. Aw! I really don't know how to start to tell you what

—Sickly—

I'm thinking is going on with him. But I tried to accept it myself and I still don't understand," says Derrick. "Derrick, could you just tell me what's going on?" asks Corey. "All right look! When we were kids, Todd used to do weird things when he was angry. If somebody bothered him, made him mad, he would stare at them, almost hypnotized. When I asked him what was wrong, he would turn to me and act as if nothing ever happened, he has no memory of being angry. He's never gotten into a fight, and my mother used to tell me that he was special but not for all the right reasons. Do you know I used to laugh at her like she was crazy, and I did it until one week ago, when we came back from that crazy house. Corey, I have never taken anyone of that stuff serious, and the one thing that I'm afraid of is that I might be right, god knows I wanna be wrong. But if I'm right, then we have a problem that not even Jesus can help us with. Trust me, this fight is gonna be a problem," says Derrick. "Derrick you've said everything but haven't got to the point yet," replies Corey. "Corey, I don't think you're listening. I just said Jesus can't help us. I missed church on Sunday, I'm going to confess now and me and my mom are gonna be home tonight praying. I think you should stop by, try to bring Todd, if he doesn't want to go, you should still come over yourself. There's something my mom would like you to have," replies Derrick. "Okay, I'm almost afraid to ask you what you think, but what I think is he needs a break from here. He was fine until he moved back here. He hasn't been the same at all. I'll give you a call when he comes around," says Corey. "Thanks, Corey," Derrick replies.

—DERRICK TILLIS—

Later that evening Todd is sitting in his favorite chair near the window, watching the leaves and the trees, when suddenly distracting him slightly, a man appears, unshaved, dressed like a preacher almost. But what strikes Todd is that he is not only smoking a cigarette, but he also seems to hold a bottle of scotch in his hand. The man gazes at Todd. Todd turns his attention to the man and slowly walks toward his front door, not taking his eyes off the gentleman. As the door opens, the man is nowhere to be found. Todd walks down his grassy lawn looking back and forth in both directions of the street only to find no one.

The following day, "Todd!!" Derrick yells at him as he's opening the door. "Todd! You feel like breakfast? I know you need a little air; you've been under the weather for a couple of days," says Derrick. "Yeah! I think so, I feel like I can eat a cow right now," replies Todd. "Okay then we'll take your car. I took the day off today, just figured we'll hang out a bit and discuss some things," replies Derrick. "I don't see any cameras, I'm just waiting for the director to yell cut," says Todd. Both Todd and Derrick drive to the diner. When reaching the diner and upon entering they pause at the entrance and look around briefly for a seat. They find a seat in the far corner next to a window, the waitress asks them will they want anything at this time, they order coffee and a newspaper.

"So, I'm gonna be straight with you Todd, we've known each other all our lives. I'm not gonna sugar coat anything, feel free to stop me at any time if I'm wrong. What's been going on with you is freaking me out man. What I saw in that house upstate was no figment of my imagination. Now I don't know if what's going

—Sickly—

on with you was just haunted, but you've been acting weird and not talking to me about anything. I told you, I believe anything you say. There is nothing you can say to me that I'll second guess, we've always had that understanding, so I need for you to tell me what's on your mind, cause I don't wanna be the only crazy one here," says Derrick. "Since you put it that way!! What if I told you I'm having blackouts? If I said I'm seeing things, feeling things, hearing voices. What if I said I woke up every day not knowing if the woman I lay next to is really the woman I love."

Todd looking past Derrick for a second to see the same man sitting across from him looking at him while holding a newspaper in his hand. The same man that he saw outside his house looking in at him. Derrick looking at Todd with curiosity, knowing that something has caught his attention, not wanting to make it obvious, Derrick looks at the reflection of the man from the window. He does not look over his shoulder.

Todd asks Derrick, "Do you know that guy?"

"What guy," Derrick asks. Derrick turns around quickly and looks in all directions knowing exactly whom Todd is referring to. So, he doesn't draw any attention. "The guy over by the counter that keeps looking over here," Todd says. "Naw! Never seen him before, why?" Derrick asks. "I saw him standing outside my house looking in yesterday and when I walked out, he was gone," replies Todd. "Looks like he could be a priest, or he took the clothes off of one," Derrick replies. Todd looking on at the gentleman as he and Derrick are preparing to leave the diner. Derrick asks when nearing the front door, next to where the man is sitting, "We're leaving already? I didn't get a chance to eat."

"I know a better place where we can get something different" says Todd.

Moments after Derrick and Todd exit the diner, Derrick tells Todd to make a detour for a block before turning into a nearby pharmacy. "I know what you're thinking and it's the same reason I wanted to leave," said Todd. "Yeah! Well, he doesn't look threatening so that's all the more reason to keep him close. So, you go up to the counter and I'll just wait right here by the door and wait for our fair-weather friend to come in," says Derrick. Todd walks up to the counter and asks the doctor for his help. The pharmacy door does not open but appearing across the street at a bus stop there, the man sitting in the diner sits at the bus stop with his eyes piercing into the pharmacy at Todd's back. While Derrick looks on, Derrick tells Todd, "Don't look now but we have company." As Todd turns around to make no direct contact with the man he walks toward the door. When he opens the door, he is subjected to approaching the man. Todd starts across the street in a minor rage.

"Todd! What are you doing? Todd gets back over here, Todd!! Todd!!" Derrick says. "Are you following me?" asks Todd to the man, while screaming through traffic. The man looks up as if he has no idea what Todd is talking about. Bystanders at the bus stop looking at each other, unsure of whom they are addressing the question to. The people start

—Sickly—

to panic as Todd approaches Derrick following behind with disbelief.

Todd grabs the man by the collar angrily. "Why the hell are you following me? Why are you following me?" Todd asks again. The man looks up and tells Todd, "I have something to tell you. I'm sorry I just wanted to be sure that it was you, I know your family I remember you," says the man. Todd slowly loosens his grip on the man's collar.

"I'm sorry if I spooked you or if I made you upset, I've been trying to find you for some time now. My name is P David. I was a priest in the Paul's Pathels church, you do not remember me, but I baptized you, I left the church a couple of years later because I had some problems. As you can see, I'm not at all equipped to do a sermon in my condition. This is my number, if you feel like talking give me a call and feel free to bring anyone along. There's a lot that we need to discuss. Todd, please have an open mind and don't think I'm crazy, cause I don't believe you are," said P. David. David was walking away from both Todd and Derrick at the moment throwing down his cigarette and taking out his liquor bottle. Todd looking on until P. David could not be seen anymore. "Hey! Come on man, let's go home. I gotta show you something," says Derrick.

Chapter 6

Later that evening Derrick, Todd and Lisa are gathering in the dining room with some pictures and books, a bible and a cloth like scroll that Lisa unrolls and sits at the table with. "How are you, Todd?" Lisa asks. "I truly don't know Lisa! I met a strange man today, you know what, never mind, tell me something, anything good," Todd says. Todd smiles nervously. "I'll tell you what you need to hear and what you already know deep inside. I'll tell you that the writings on the wall aren't words son, and I want you to tell me something, I want you to read this cloth and tell me what it says because I can't read it. But it was given to me by a priest a long time ago, back when you were both babies. He said that we're all here as a plan to hold something sacred together and some things shall not pass, and he also asked that I show this to no one. He who reads this, is he who we must pray for, so I want you to read this, and if you can understand it, tell me what you wish, if not, then we'll deal with what's going on with all of us, day by day, step by step, can we do that?" asks Lisa. Todd looks at Lisa and slowly grabs the cloth and unrolls it very hesitantly. He frowns, looking back and forth at what seems to be margins of words to him, but signs and scribble and numbers to Lisa's eyes and whomever else that may set their sights on it. "Son, can you tell me what this means?" asks

—Sickly—

Lisa. Todd puts the scroll away and sits back in the chair and looks at both Derrick and Lisa and says, "No!!" Lisa stares Todd in his eyes to see the sweat dripping down his cheek. "Todd you really have no idea what this means?!" Derrick asks. Todd answers, "No!!"

"Okay than, I would like you to look at this chapter in this book, this book has no cover, it's not a bible because no one believe that all the truths and beliefs of different religions coincide with each other. But they all have the same meaning, the priest that gave me this book wrote the first page as a diary, he gave me this book thirty-three years ago. The first entry was in 1732, over 200 years ago. He was denounced from his ministry because the higher priests in the church believed that he would poison the minds of the people with his going on about his beliefs. He didn't fear death, he embraced the idea of the coming. Then after a couple years, I noticed that I was waking up to see my husband die and my boy grow, and what struck me the most is the priest. People get old and they change, but he didn't look a day past the time I first met him. I haven't seen him in almost fifteen years, but the things that were written in this book are what made me keep it. Now I don't know if he wanted me to believe that he wrote everything in this book, but a child is mentioned here, and a grey days and dark nights are also mentioned. And the reader of times to come will bring forth the laws of the new system. If any of this makes sense to you, you may have this book, and you may have this scroll and we will never have this talk again. Just remember, in your worst of times, I'll always

—DERRICK TILLIS—

be there for you," Lisa said to Todd. "Okay!! Well, I gotta get goin, I'm meeting Corey at her friend's house for dinner tonight, um, Derrick if your free tonight?" asks Todd. "Naw! You go ahead man. Have fun, I have a couple of things I need to do tonight, talk to you soon," replies Derrick. Todd stands up preparing to leave, Derrick doesn't see him off, Lisa hugs him. Todd knowing that Derrick is upset and doubts he's telling the whole truth, he drops his head walking out the door with his car keys in hand.

Derrick remembers that he has the number that was given to Todd from David and leans back on his bed staring at the ceiling. Derrick jumps up and grabs the phone and dials the number slowly. Suddenly, "Hello," said P. David. "I want to know everything you know about Todd," Derrick says. "Derrick, right? I was expecting this call. But I would rather meet in person, and please come alone, but if you do not want the truth, may I suggest that you don't come at all," P. David replies. "Where do you wanna meet?" Derrick asks. "The church on North Broadway, come at noon tomorrow. If you're a minute late you'll be going for forgiveness cause I won't be there," P. David says. "I'll be there, you just make sure you are," Derrick replies. Derrick hangs up the phone and walks over to the window. The sky is dark and grey with no rain, the trees don't sway, there is no breeze, and there aren't any animals visible, not a bird in sight. Derrick pulls his curtains down and lays his head on his pillow with his hands folded under his head, he drifts off into a light sleep.

Chapter 7

The following day Derrick prepares to meet with P. David. As he's leaving Lisa asks, "Good morning, so where should I assume you're off to?"

"I gotta go meet with someone mom, I won't be gone long," Derrick replies. "Derrick, may I suggest that you don't go any further with this, and get yourself all caught up in something that may not be healthy for you son," Lisa says. "Mom I've been acting like I don't know what's going on around, serving the justice system, and protecting the innocent, following the rules and regulations of the law. I feel like I just exist sometimes, like everything around me is just a part of a plan, like I've been a part of a plan, and I don't know who's footprints are placed in the sand to carry me as far as I would like to believe I've come. But if I need to change a couple of things on my journey into the Netherlands, then I need to start moving now. Mom, Todd is in hell and with me. I can't get any answers because he's not opening up to me, but if I choose to find out for myself what's going on with my friend, my brother, I need to go at it alone, with no obstacles. Now I ask that you just trust me and let me do this, let me see what you see mom," Derrick says. Lisa, looking at Derrick with a view of encouragement, proud, she says nothing! "I'll call you when I'm on my way home ma! I Love You" Derrick says.

—DERRICK TILLIS—

Derrick turning to walk out the door, as it closes Lisa sees her son, she sees his father she sees herself.

Lisa walks toward the window to see her son leaving, suddenly the phone rings!

Lisa turns her attention to the phone. "Hello," says Lisa. There is no answer, and then suddenly a voice says, "Hello." Lisa asks, "Hello, may I ask who's' calling?"

"Hello ma'am my name is Jason. Is Derrick available?" asks Jason. "No, but can I take a message?" Lisa asks. "Naw, but thanks, I'll call again some other time, you have a good day now," Jason says.

Lisa hanging up the phone and turns towards the kitchen and hears the creaking of footsteps upstairs. She freezes and looks towards her Bible with an uncomfortable ease. "Father, I believe in you, I know you're with me at all times," Lisa says to herself. But before she can finish there's a voice, a very deep voice. A voice that is felt. "I hope for your sake he hears your cries. I hope he answers you before the worst happens. I hope you have made peace with all of your sins. I will kill you woman." Lisa closes her eyes and places her hand on her chest to pray and slowly whispers. But before she finishes, the form of a shadow appears in front of her, she stops and slowly opens her eyes and without a sound she tears. Staring into the face of someone, something she only knew existed in her heart, it is what she feared the most. Lisa says, "God if you are here, I am safe." The house starts to rumble, the eyes that she's staring into causes her to lose consciences briefly. Falling and holding her heart, she looks over at her sons'

—Sickly—

picture and says softly, "Derrick I'm sorry, I love you!!" And with her final and last words, Lisa is no more.

With Derrick racing to meet with P. David, and with Corey and Todd off to see friends, the sky suddenly starts to darken, with no warning of rain or weather condition, Derrick looks on and says, "Now I know something is wrong. This is bullshit and I can't shake these butterflies. Meanwhile father P. David awaiting Derrick outside the church, the sky is grey. He puts out his cigarette to enter through the back of the church, briefly looks around before opening the door. Derrick arrives not a minute late. He looks around before he pulls the front doors open with caution. As he enters the church, he finds P. David sitting in front of the church.

"So, you made it on time and I'm sure you're wondering about the gloomy dressed sky, never mind it. What's coming, neither you nor I may be able to stop it," P. David says. "I'm almost afraid to ask what it is we need to stop, but as I said almost," Derrick replies. "Son, do you know what's going on around you? Do you know who you're dealing with? In the first book, there was a man named Jason. Jason wrote the book of the greatest stories ever told. He was young, and very intuitive, but he was also easily influenced. Rules didn't apply to him as he saw it, he was a free spirit, always looking for the easier route. Do you know how old I am?" asks P. David. "I would like to say around fifty-five, but I'm afraid you gonna tell me you're a lot older," Derrick replies. "I don't remember. I can remember every day of my life but the day of my birth, or my age. But the real question is what you really need to

—DERRICK TILLIS—

know, do you really want to know the truth about your friend?" P. David asks. "I think we both know why I'm here so if you would," Derrick replies. "Your friend isn't who you think he is, actually he never was. Where I'm from when you lose your memory, it's a result of massive trauma, like your head broke in two, or in his case the fact that he was tossed into the abyss for a sin that was unforgiven," P. David stated. "Wait!! What do you mean, thrown into the abyss and unforgiving sin?" Derrick asks. "Did you not understand? What you think right now is what you should be thinking. Yes!! Exactly everything that just crossed your mind is what you should be preparing yourself for. I knew your mother a long time ago, I gave her something, something of value. I told her to give it to the one she believed that can read the writings on the wall and understand them. Your mother was a great woman," P. David says. Derrick slightly frowns and asks, "What do you mean she was a great woman? "You talk as if she's dead," Derrick says. Church bell sounding. "I need to leave now, you can reach me when the sun is at its greatest," P. David says. "Hold on, what the hell do you mean? And what about my mother?" Derrick asks. "I'm sorry, but I have to go now. I'm sorry for your loss, truly," P. David says. "Is that it? What is it that's missing here?" Derrick asks. P. David hastily walked toward the rear exit of the church, not to utter another word. Leaving Derrick standing beside the podium to see him leave.

Chapter 8

"Todd, could you grab the coffee cake from the backseat for me hun? "Oh, and try not to drop it," Corey says. "Corey doesn't the sun look a bit off?" Todd asks. "Honey the sun isn't out, is everything ok?" Corey asks. Todd looking into the sky, Todd and Corey don't seem to see the same things at the moment. He starts getting worried. "Honey!! If we can, you know, sway on up the stairs now," Corey says. "Yeah, I'm right behind you," Todd replies. Corey and Todd both enter the door at Susan's house to be greeted by some mutual acquaintances. "Corey, I think we need to talk after everyone is gone. There are some strange things happening that I don't understand, and you might not either," Susan says. Susan and Corey both leaving the kitchen after being briefly interrupted by Todd. "So, what's going on?" Todd asks. Both Corey and Susan answer, "Oh nothing."

Derrick tried to call home to his mom, while getting no answer after numerous attempts, he starts to worry. While racing home, he feels the need to call Todd, unfortunately Todd left the phone in the car. "Damn it, Todd! Pick up, okay, okay! Call home," Derrick mumbles to himself. Derrick calls home again with no answer. Cell phone in one hand and Onstar still not responding. Derrick's phone rings, "Hello, hello!" he says. "Hello, Derrick, how have you been? This is

—DERRICK TILLIS—

Jason," he says. "Jason why am I not surprised," Derrick stated. "First, I think you need to get home before allowing other things to distract you that are out of your control. Second, I think that what you think you know may not be beneficial to you or those you love. And third, don't bother with Todd, he's about to wake up any day now. He's been sleep for a while and you have a pleasant evening," Jason says. "Hello, Hello, Jason? Hello," Derrick says. The phone hangs up, Derrick just pulling up to the front of his home. He yells out, "Mom, Mom." Derrick is frantic, he opens the door and runs inside, "Mom," he yells out again, and just as he turns to go up the stairs, he finds his mom on the floor, eyes wide open. "Mom, mom, get up mom, mom get up we need to go to the hospital," Derrick says. "Mom" Derrick yells while kneeling to her. "Mom" Derrick says again. Derrick whispers for the last time, finally accepting that Lisa is gone. He lays beside his mother, closing her eyes, smiling while the tears are running down his cheek. He does not move, cradled next to her like a baby cradled next to his mother.

"Susan is everything okay? You've been acting weird since we've got here" Corey says. "Trust me Corey, it's not you but I don't think you see what's happening around us. I'm afraid Corey, and you and Todd act as if nothing happened on our trip" Susan replies. "I understand! The house spooked you or maybe that guy Jason was playing tricks on us but I'm afraid of a few ghosts' stories" Corey says. "I don't think you understand or maybe you just don't wanna except the fact that you as well as Todd and myself may have a problem," Susan

—Sickly—

replies. Corey growing upset and decides to leave, she refuses to stay for the remainder of the evening. "Honey grab your coat, I forgot I have a couple of things I need to do home" Corey says to Todd. "Okay. What happened? Did I miss something? We just got here an hour ago" Todd stated. "I just wanna go home" Corey replies. "Okay, Susan thanks for the hospitality and it was nice to meet you all. Good evening!" Todd said. With Corey and Todd leaving, Susan looks out of the window, almost afraid. She knows there's something wrong but doesn't know exactly what.

"Corey is there something you're not telling me? I mean you asked me to come to this party, but you haven't said anything to me since we got there and you and Susan seem to be at each other's throats, and when I walk in, you both get quiet" Todd says. "Well Todd I apologize if I'm not myself lately, but you haven't been all together and besides that, ever since we've come back here you've been acting weird. I've been listening to you, Derrick and Lisa babble about craziness and church stories and not once have you asked if I'm okay or how I'm dealing with what's going on with us" Corey replies. Todd doesn't say a word, his phone rings. "Todd, can you answer the phone for once!! Can you listen to me for once?" Corey says.

"Hello" Todd answers. "Todd I'm pregnant" Corey says. "My mom," Derrick whispers. "Todd did you hear me?" Corey asks. Both Derrick and Corey, both repeating themselves again. "My mother's gone Todd" Derrick says. "Todd I'm pregnant"

47

—DERRICK TILLIS—

Corey says. Todd drops the phone and stops the car at a red light, eyes wide open, in shock.

At the funeral, Derrick looks at the coffin that his mother is inside with a blank expression on his face, while Todd stands beside him, eyes watery but he will not cry. Family and friends look on and mourn the loss of their friend, family, sister, co-worker.

Beyond the trees there stands the priest P. David looking on, he sheds a single tear, there is more hurt in his face than in her own sons' eyes, Todd sees him. Todd suddenly starts toward the trees that P. David is found peeking from behind, Derrick picks up his head to see that Todd is walking away. As Todd gets closer, P. David leaves. Todd is left standing, and P. David is nowhere to be found.

"Mom, I should have listened to you" Derrick says. Derrick speaks out into the sky with a bottle of alcohol in his hand and his gun on his shoulder. "You always told me to go to church, pray, and do my homework. All of the things you're supposed to be here to see your grandchild do" Derrick says.

While Derrick sits outside, Todd stares from the window. "So, are you gonna go to him? I think you should, we'll be here when you get back" Corey says to Todd.

Todd walking out of his front door, Derrick picks his head up. "Mom look, Todd is coming over, Todd mom said you should come to church with us on Sunday" Derrick says. "O' yeah" Todd replies. "Yeah, and she also said that you got a secret, a secret so bad that you don't even know about…

—Sickly—

Todd? Do you have a secret you're not sharing or are you burying it so damn deep that you truly don't know shit??" Derrick asks Todd while drunk with tears in his eyes, and a smile on his face. "I don't know anything anymore Derrick. I don't care to find out anymore. Can you give me that? I lost my family, I lost the only real mom I've ever known, I have one brother still here, and can something be normal for once?" Todd replies.

Derrick looking at Todd without a word. Todd stands up and starts to make his way back across the street. Derrick asks softly, "So what are you gonna name the baby?"

"I don't know, I was thinking about naming him Junior, you have a name in mind?" Todd asks. "Naw! Not right now, but we'll figure something out" Derrick says. Derrick looking on as Todd turns and heads back towards his house. Deep down inside he knows that his mother's death may possibly have something to do with his best friend.

As Derrick gets up to enter his home, he stops before grabbing the doorknob and says, "I'm not good at what I do because I graduated college."

"Bravo!! Bravo!! Now tell me something" says Jason. "What??" Derrick asks. "I think we had this talk already if I'm not mistaken but do you know who? Oh Yeah! You call him Todd! Do you know what Todd's responsibility is? Let me rephrase that, do you know who Todd really is and why you two can't play in the sandbox anymore?" Jason says. Derrick slowly turns around to the mysterious man who stands beneath the stairs. "I know Todd, but whatever you know

—DERRICK TILLIS—

about him, or whatever you think you know, I suggest you keep it to yourself" Derrick says. "Again, this isn't something you turn on or off because you made him a physical figment of family, you've grown to love him as if you have the option. His destiny is inevitable. He will do what he needs to when he wants to do so, nor you or I can change his mind, trust me, it'll be great. Just as Derrick reaches for his gun, Jason disappears, leaving Derrick at his doorstep.

Derrick turns around to open his door and enters only to find P. David standing with his back to him in the living room. "How the hell did you get in here and what do you what?" Derrick asks. "Well, I would like to tell you that the door was open but that would be a lie, and I don't lie" P. David says. "So, what is it that you want?" Derrick asks again. "I want you to help me help you. I don't think you understand just how dangerous this has become nor do you respect the principles of the rules that apply" P. David says. "Listen, I lost my mom, when I left home, she was in perfectly good health, and when I came back, she was laid out on the floor as pale as a ghost. Now can you tell me how or why everything seems to be tumbling down around me for? If Todd has the big secret or the problem, why is it affecting me? Why did my mother have to die?" Derrick asks. "All that you know is outta the hands of your father now, all that you know is not of God anymore. Don't you see?? It's all from something bad! It was all written, you were all part of this, you're all part of a bigger picture, whether you want this or not" P. David replies.

—Sickly—

Before P. David could finish, Derrick interrupts. "Just before I walked in, I saw Jason and for some reason," Derrick said. "You saw who?" P. David asks with surprise, after cutting Derrick off. "I saw Jason outside my door, he wanted to talk" Derrick said.

P. David rushed to the window to peek outside only to find that Jason was no longer around. "Whatever you do you must not allow Jason to influence you in any kind of way, he must not be allowed to tell you what you already know" P. David said. "I don't understand anything you're saying right now" Derrick replies. "Listen to me!!" P. David shouts at Derrick in panic. "He is the reason that all of you are going through what you've been going through. He convinced the son to go against the father, his brother. He uses influences over your future, your past, anything traumatic in your life and he feeds on it. Makes it black and uses it, Jason is Todd's link" P. David says. "Can I ask you a question Dave?" Derrick asks. "Yes, anything," P. David replies. "Is Todd who he thinks he is?" Derrick asks. "No! Son, Todd lost his memory many years ago when we were all dismounted from our high posts in what you call Heaven. In what you now are confused about, the questions in your mind are all true, you believe then, so you see everything. Todd was born and raised again but Todd is not awake yet, you'll see. Once he remembers who he is, I'm afraid that everything you both know and love is lost" P. David says. Derrick looking at P. David as if someone took away all that means everything to him and Derrick asks, "What is the reason for me, Susan, Corey, my mom and everything and everybody around us to feel what Todd is going through? Will he get his memory back?"

"I'm afraid he isn't far from it now, all it will take is for him to go through something traumatic to trigger the happening and unfortunately, Jason knows that and knows his weakness" P. David replies. "I gotta find him, I gotta find him now!!" Derrick says. "I'm going with you" P. David says. Both P. David and Derrick walking out the door. Just when it starts to rain very heavily!!

Chapter 9

"We both know who Jason will be after, don't we?" P. David says. P. David and Derrick both looking on to the road while speeding at a rate of 90 mph and Derrick turns to P. David and says, "Todd will listen to me."

"You don't sound too sure" P. David says. "At this point I'm not but he doesn't have much of a choice. But this is not about him anymore, this is bigger than all of us" Derrick says.

Derrick calls Todd at this point, while the phone is ringing there's a knock at the door. "Honey, could you get that?" Corey asks. "Yeah! You get the phone while I get the door" Todd replies. "I can't, I'm in the shower" Corey says. "Okay I'll get both" Todd says. Todd grabs the phone while reaching for the door at the same time.

"Hello" Todd asks and grabs the handle on the front door. "I'm coming over now" Derrick says. "You don't sound too good, what's going on?" Todd asks. The door is opening at this time and Jason appears to be standing in front of Todd. "Hey Todd, long time no see! I told Derrick to let you know I'll be stopping by" Jason says. Todd was looking with curiosity at Jason with the phone still in his ear. "Todd closes the door, close the door Todd" Derrick says. "Too late for that now, hand me the phone" Jason says to Todd. Jason snatches the phone from Todd pushing him back, very easily lifting him

—DERRICK TILLIS—

off of his feet into the air. He lands in the corner breaking the flower stand. "Todd!!" Derrick screams into the phone, almost nearing the house, just blocks away. "Damn, Damn, Shit!!" Derrick says. "This can go wrong in so many ways" P. David says. Jason smiles and puts the phone to his ear to speak. "Todd, I thought I told you that this is just not the right course in life for you. "Listen, if you put a hand on him" Derrick starts to say, but before he could finish with his empty threats Jason says, "Too late. I already put a hand on him and he's out for the count, but not to worry because he gathers no bumps or bruises trust me. But you on the other hand, my friend can be put to rest. See I can't hurt my mentor, but I have figured out a way to wake him up. He will be angry in the beginning, but, Oh' when the end is near everyone will be happy, or sad in your case. But my friend, I think I'll have to take a rain check on your anger issues and concerns, I have a date with a pretty blonde who is upstairs taking a shower. Bye now!!"

Jason hangs up before Derrick can utter another word, Todd still unconscious and Corey in the shower. "Here we go!! Here we go!!" Derrick says. Jason slowly walks up the stairs singing to himself with a voice that isn't his own. Derrick jumps out of the door with David and yells out loudly looking up at the window, thinking Corey. Jason slowly opens the bathroom door to find Corey drying her hair, Corey says "Hey hun, I was just, Ahh!!" Corey screams, the panic causes Derrick to kick the door in and also waking Todd from his unfortunate plunder. Derrick runs past Todd and up the

—Sickly—

stairs. "Corey" Derrick screams. "Honey!?" Todd says. Todd jumps up and races up the stairs, from room to room. He searches every room, once he enters the bathroom, he finds nothing but writing in the mirror. It says, "If you wish to see this bitch again, you'll come to the house, you know where!!" "What the hell? Why?" Todd asks.

Todd turns his attention to David, and in a rage, he slams him against the wall and asks, "Why is this happening, she has nothing to do with this. Whatever I'm going through is because of me, so you need to tell me something."

"All I can say is that if you're strong enough to handle your losses, then you must prepare yourself for what's to come and let's get to her before he makes up his mind about her" David says. "What do you mean" Todd asks. "I mean, the worst possible things known to man, so try not to think about any of them right now" David replies. "Okay, enough talk, let's go and Todd" Derrick says. Todd turned to see what Derrick wanted. "I just might have to shoot you, and I won't hesitate" Derrick says. "And what the hell does that mean Derrick" Todd asks angrily. "Well, it means that you might decide to do something that we both know is wrong for all the right reasons. I just lost my mother, I don't need you turning on me at the stroke of midnight" Derrick replies. Todd and Derrick both looking into each other's eyes, before leaving out the front door. But in a distant remote area Corey is held, not bonded but sits in a chair, wondering, afraid and curious as to why she is here. Jason enters the room with a Bible in hand and speaks softly.

—DERRICK TILLIS—

"Have you ever read the Bible Corey? You ever read the Bible to know the truth or were you forced to go hear the word because that's what your parents did? You know I've never read the Bible. It would upset me after a while because I couldn't understand who was telling the stories. I mean, there's no one around to see what you're doing but everyone knows what's going to come or what you're up to. Do you know who I am Corey?" Jason asks. "You're Jason, but I don't understand why you're doing this" Corey replies. Jason screams, frightening Corey, "Do you know who I am? Do you know why I'm here? And most importantly, do you know Todd, as you would call him. I don't think so Corey, I really don't. I'm going to read you a passage in this book and then you can tell me if you know anything at all. This is the original book of my fathers, And it reads, and I quote, *"My son, my flesh, my image will be onto thee, take heed to his word, and his warning of the days to come. I have given choice, fare as my heart, but I will be the only being that you shall worship,"* funny huh? My father was never recognized for all the good that he sought to bring. He was never given the attention that his brother would be given, like Kane and Able. Once you decide who's good, you've already made up your mind about who's bad. And what are you to do when the one thing you're good at is not what you want to be doing? You know I think we should get down to business and not prolong the baffle and mayhem, I would love for you to witness." Corey's voice trembling in fear as she asks Jason, "What do you want from us?"

—Sickly—

"Us? Who? You and Todd? Nothing at all, I'm just waiting for the love of your life to crack the shell so we can get down to business, real business, grown up stuff. You had your fun playing the all-American family, now we need to finish what we were intended to do since the beginning. We are going to wage war, I D Clare War!!" Jason replies. Jason laughs critically as if it were a game that was never going to end.

"I have something I need to give you Todd" David says. "I don't think right now is a good time to be exchanging any gifts Dave," Derrick says. "I think right now is the perfect time son!" David replies. David sitting in the backseat looking in the rear-view mirror into Derricks eyes awaiting eye contact. Derrick suddenly looks up and notices David trying to tell him something, but at the moment he cannot turn his attention off the road at the rate of speed he's going. David looking at the back of Todd's head, wide eyed, almost frozen, peers of red and blonde streaks are aligned on his scalp, his hair slightly changed color in one area of his head, then suddenly…

"Can you speed up? You're a cop for Christ sakes!!" Todd says. "Todd, I think you need to calm down," Derrick replies. "I am calm, this is me calm" Todd replies back. "Todd, are you feeling okay because you need to have a clear head, Jason has a hidden agenda that is not so hidden and you're the only one that seems to be in the dark about this," P. David says. "Listen, he has my wife. I don't understand what you think I'm thinking right about now, but she's pregnant and she's in no position to be dealing with what she's been dealing with

—DERRICK TILLIS—

since we've been back. Can you find prayer in that? Can our father in heaven help my circumstances now?" Todd asks. "You know what son, if you believed in the father from the beginning, I could tell you none of us would be in the positions were in today, you were given a choice as were man," David said.

Derrick looking at David through the rear view, only to see him angrily looking off into the dark of the night. Todd not responding but Derrick knowing exactly what David meant. "Can I ask you something Dave?" Derrick asks. Derrick glaring through the rear view at P. David. "Sure, and you're not the one who needs to know why I said what I said. But you seem to be the one that pays the most attention," David says. "What do you mean?" Todd asks. "Oh! You didn't catch that little given choice speech just now. When will the third party come Dave? Me, you, him, us, man and who else?" Derrick asks. "He knows who else, if anyone in this car knows what this is about it would be you. You are a man of admiration to your friends and family, and yet, you don't have a clue about you," David says. "What about me? What about me, you son of a bitch? Why is everything such an obstacle, a puzzle?" Todd asks.

Nearing the location of the church, Todd finds himself a bit familiar with the wooded area. The church has been abandoned for many years. The car pulls up to the gate where the vines have drowned out the original design of the walls and the fountain that poured water into the cracks of concrete in the scriptures on the pavement was dry. Todd is the first

—Sickly—

one out of the car, David the second, and Derrick slowly opens the car door carefully, looking on in suspense, almost frightened. With curiosity Todd moves toward the gate where the vines seem to sickle as if they were afraid.

Todd pushes the gate open, the old vines and leaves break away like dead leaves. David drops his book on the ground and begins to breathe heavily and fast.

"Like I said before son, if you didn't believe in your father before, now would be a great time because you have no idea what your about to start. You must be graceful and pure, even in your sleep, so you are vast and careful when you're awake," David says. With the day dimming to darkness faster than usual, in the distance you can hear a whisper; the whisper catches Todd's attention quickly, he looks around to see if anyone was aware of what he just heard, then David turns to him and asks, "Do you hear it? Can you feel the energy around you?" Derrick pulls his gun out and aims into the mist and asks, "Hear what? Somebody talk to me, if you two are hearing things I want to know what they're saying."

"You wouldn't understand, only Todd and I understand, and pretty soon he'll be the only one that can hear it at all. This is what I was afraid of," David replies. "So how do you stop it? Well? How do we stop it?" Derrick asks impatiently. "We can't, we just need to hope that he makes the right decision for his family," David replies. "Todd, it looks like you have some decisions to make, I hope we're on the same page bro!" Derrick says. Todd off into a slight trans, as If he's

—DERRICK TILLIS—

left his body behind and went somewhere else. Then suddenly out of the mist Jason and Corey appear.

"Todd, I really don't think we have time to find yourself, you've never been so far outta you head, it's almost sickening. Come back to us for a moment, even if you can't convince yourself. Tsk, tsk, tsk, all that influence, you're going to be some kind of mad."

Jason says to Todd. Jason laughs slightly while holding Corey's neck, and Corey being bound to a chair with ropes. Suddenly Todd comes out of his trans, the cross on his neck begins to slightly bend and turn black from its wooded figure as if it were being burned. "Corey, are you okay?" Todd asks his wife. Corey crying trying to free herself and cursing at Jason, saying "Let me go you son of a bitch!" Jason laughing hysterically." And if either of you take one step further this bitch's head will meet you halfway into your journey," Jason says. "Jason look, let her go, she has nothing to do with his" Todd says. "I beg to differ, see she has a lot to do with the fact that I'm here where I shouldn't be and you're not where you should be. See you bumped your head kind of hard and forgot everything. Quite frankly I'm getting tired of playing these games. This is the main event, and if Derrick doesn't put that fucking gun away, God help him, I will shove it in his mother rotten corpse after I'm done ripping his arms off," Jason says angrily. "Todd let me shoot him, let me shoot him Todd" says Derrick. "It won't work soon, you know it won't and you also know calling his bluff won't help either, Todd it's up to you," David says. "Jason, what do you want from

—Sickly—

me?" Todd asks. The clouds turning burgundy red, the sun looks as if it's bleeding with the moon sneaking up at the same time, all in motion. Jason's voice changes, he begins to speak. "This is what I want from you Todd, I want to savor this moment right here." And with a blink of an eye, Corey begins to bleed. Her eyes look as if they're bleeding with tears. "What are you doing to her stop," Todd yells while running towards Corey. "I told you not to come any closer," Jason said.

And with a swift swing of the rusted shovel in hand, Jason almost loses his balance keeping his threat as promised. All three looking on, David being the only one not in shock, he closes his eyes and bows his head as the rain begins.

"No, Corey," Todd yells out in pain. Derrick opens his mouth and runs toward Jason, and with a thrust he is thrown through the gardens fountain into the waterless cracking ground. Todd dropping to his knees crying looking on, with his hands to his side, Todd softly whispers his wife's name once more, "Corey."

"Now we're moving along, snap out of it, you're embarrassing me," Jason says.

Jason walks over grabbing Todd by the collar and dragging him, his body almost lifeless, then suddenly, his hair starts to slowly turn red, his eyes begin to change color, an orange color, his skin collects an onslaught of veins, he inhales as if he just pulled himself out of water, he quickly shakes loose Jason pulling himself forward onto his feet as if lost. Todd takes a deep breath, picks his head up and looks at where his wife once sat on the chair where her body lies now and her

—DERRICK TILLIS—

head at his feet, he looks down at his wife without a sound. The passing of the wind, clouds, sun, and moon, slow down to almost frozen. A bird flies over his head, dashes down and gently sit on Todd's shoulder. He turns his attention to the bird while his friend Derrick picks himself up from the gravel that Jason embedded him in. Todd asks the bird if he had a name as if they were the only two presents in the garden. David says nothing as he looks on at Todd with his eyes looking at such sorrow, a sorrow that can't be explained. Derrick climbed out of the gravel to see his best friend in a subtle and peaceful state of mind.

Jason asking Todd, "Are we all together now?"

"How would you like to be rewarded?" Todd asks. "Rewarded? I have waited for years to find you, I have bent the rules and actually put what your enemy would call faith into you, and that is what you ask," Jason replies. "If you know me Jason, truly know me then you'd know I have never spoken of faith, maybe fate, but never hope, and I have grown to live, to love something other than my own. Why would you want thee to be other than what I was?" Todd asks. "Listen!! You bumped your head really hard and disappeared for centuries," Jason said. "I was never gone, only living for a moment in time, I wanted to understand what this is, to be," Todd says.

"You still have a choice," David says. Todd turns his attention to Jason while the bird flies away and David slowly pulls out the book, he has been holding for most of his existence. "Look Todd, this is our freedom, submission to

—Sickly—

him, we can be free," David says. "No, you cannot!! You are a fool and he who has set the prints in the sand will forbid any further broken promises from the last one, the deal was done," Jason says. "And Jason, you are absolutely right. David, I apologize if you're not getting through to me right now but the woman, I've grown to love is at my feet, I can still hear her. Do you know what she's saying right now, even in death while she's looking up at me?" Todd asks. "Yes, I do! But you just have to understand it all can be rewritten," David replies. "Sorry David, but your faith in me held you captive all of your existence. Whose side did you expect I'd be on? There are 2 sides, and we both know that what has happen lately only tells you what side I'm on," Todd says.

"Todd!!" Derrick yells out. "I understand, but I know you, you're angry right now," Derrick says. "Say my name," Todd asks. Derrick stops and looks at Todd in curiosity. "Listen I don't know," Derrick replies. Interrupted by Todd, Todd says again, "Say my name!!" Derrick starts to fear, he knows now who his friend, his brother, his partner, the closest person to him is telling him to do something against his faith.

"Look at the bright side, there aren't any moments like this ever, Adam was the only other person that got to meet me, through Eve, now if you love me like you think you do, you'll tell me what my real name is, tell the truth Derrick, cause we know what happens to a liar. Derrick looking on at Todd, David looking at Derrick and Jason with a smile on his face of uncertainty. Todd asks again, "Derrick what is my name?"

—DERRICK TILLIS—

"Lucifer, that's your name" Derrick replies. "Now can we skip the shenanigans?" Jason asks.

And with a raise of his hand, Todd turns to Jason, picking him up into the air and says, "And you were supposed to be born, not kill your mother, you were supposed to be here later, not now, I have no use for you if she cannot be, and if so my son, neither can you. Stay still this won't hurt a bit." With the closing of his fists, Jason bursts into ashes. "Ashes to ashes, dust to dust, and back to the nothing you have become. "Todd please!! There is another way," David says.

"You know David, I never faulted you for your faith in him, but know this, I will not let you get in my way for any reason, and you can live on this earth for as long you so shall see fit, eternal life, who doesn't want that? But his route you've chosen we know where it will end up, so I think I'll be on my merry way, and you can stand here with my best friend and figure things out, oh and Derrick, you have the option, I mean who'd know that your best friend would turn out to be your worst enemy. Bu I am not your enemy, because I love you!! Yep, I love you, I love you more than anyone else on this miserable planet, I love her the same, so the choice is yours. Even when I'm not around, I'm always around, just look over your shoulder. People are given choices, and when they make a choice 90% of the time it's in my favor, who says the world is perfect," Todd says while inhaling deeply.

"I can still hear your mother speaking to me; I can help you listen, to hear her asking me to let you be. I love you too mom, hey she won't say she loves me back. Should I feel bad

—Sickly—

about that Derrick? You know I never had a mom, I just seemed to exist, and it's been so long I can't even tell you where it all started, humph!! I wonder if he made us as he made you, in his own image, never trust beauty, I was the most handsome to ever exist, my only sin was that I had my own ideas, too much of a thinker," Todd says. "Todd, can we talk a bit?" Derrick asks. "Derrick it's too late," David says. Todd walking towards the gates, metal swaying like the vines that inhabited them. "Derrick!! You are my brother, remember that and remember I have only loved a number of times and have been betrayed only once," Todd says. "Todd, Todd, where are you going?" Derrick asks. "Again, my name isn't Todd, you call me by my name," Todd replies. "Your name is Todd!!" Derrick says. With Todd exiting the gate to no longer be seen walking away in the midst, Derrick slowly loses conciseness, going into a faint, almost deep sleep.

Pastor David awakening Derrick from his faint moment and tells him, "I've tried for years to find good within myself and to find where I went wrong in all my endeavors. I know now that it is not my mission to pursue Todd; I know now that it is yours; he has lost everything and everyone dear to him but one. That one person is you and if you could believe enough in yourself to see that you may not only change the circumstances, but you may be able to ring him back to that place where he found peace.

"He's been my friend all my life, he's been a brother to me, I don't know where his faith any my faith made a difference in all this, I mean we went to church together, we prayed together, and for my brother to become my enemy wouldn't be something you just wake up one day and decide would happen, I hesitated to pull the trigger, I hesitated," Derrick says.

"Even if you would have pulled that trigger you wouldn't have done anything but upset him even more. Derrick listen, he has no intention on killing you unless you force his hand, and son, I am truly sorry to tell you that I cannot give you the answers on how to do so," David replies.

"Where is he headed?" Derrick asks.

"To Babylon, but you call it, New York City. You see bright lights and tourists and a place that everyone in the world wants to see, some before Disneyland. Do you know what we see son through our eyes? Beneath your grounds and bright lights, there is an ancient ground, buried beneath. It is the remains of a tower, it was forbidden by the father, it was nurtured and built with the blood and sweat of all the nations, there was a time when all men were of one nation under God, yes, we all spoke in one language, until man coming into his nature thought that by building this tower of uselessness, they'd find God. There was a great storm, that in which destroyed the tower and many others, at that time Todd was not yet ready to be born again, he was lost, yet leaving all of his followers in limbo, I was one, I choose another path, the path that would help me to regain salvation in my own mind because I felt hope again. If you want to stop this hell you must have faith and keep hope, believe in yourself as God

—*Sickly*—

believed in his children. Never doubt him, now we must hurry back to the city and find Todd," David says.

With both David and Derrick gathering themselves to go back to New York, the skies have yet to clear. Derrick stared at the car with a deep breath as if he were preparing himself for something he thought he may never be the same from, while leaving his gun behind with a knowing of its uselessness.

Chapter 10

Derrick and P. David arrive back at Derrick's home, hesitant to enter his home with the yellow caution tape and broken furniture still in place from what previously haunted him. The mother that he lost and facing the grim events still stuck in his mind. He takes a deep breath before walking back inside his front door with P. David lighting a cigarette and looking up at the sky in a scared and wondrous gaze, he yells out!!

"Derrick, we have to go, we must go now Derrick, he started the cycle, we need to leave," David says. P. David entering the home to rush Derrick out. "What do you suppose I do? I mean who made the decision for me to be the one to save the world, I mean really, this is stuff you only see in movies and read in books. I'm not a savior, I'm not the chosen one, it's not like I have a manual or there's something in the Bible to tell me how to approach this and with my mother gone…" Derrick says.

Derrick looking down at the spot where his mother last lay, with a tear running down his cheek. "I can't say I know how you feel, I've never had a mother, but you need to pull yourself together son, there's still a chance for you, I don't have that option, my time here is just about over. So please pull it together! Please, just try, that's all I ask, don't let her

— *Sickly* —

death be in vain. He cannot win, and maybe if you had a little faith, something may change, maybe he will hear your cries and help, but you have to be strong son," P. David says.

Derrick looking over his shoulder at P. David, as if his confidence was his mother's own. Derrick asks, "Where can I find him?" P. David putting out the cigarette says, "He's going where all his followers are and they don't even know it."

"And where is that?" Derrick asks. "New York City," P. David replies.

Forty-five minutes later Derrick and P. David arrive to New York. Awkwardly P. David is distraught by what he sees. Derrick asks, "What's wrong? I don't like that look. Dave talks to me,"

"It's started!!" P. David responds. P. David bending down to both knees to pray. "What's started, do you feel something I don't" Derrick asks. "Our father who art in heaven, save us from," P. David says. But before David can finish, he is caught with a slight strain and nosebleed.

"Alright, there's something you're not saying, and I need to know," Derrick says.

P. David opens his eyes before Derrick can finish his sentence, he inhales deeply, eyes turning bloodshot red and yellow and says, "Boy, run!!"

"I'm not running from anything," Derrick says. P. David back from the land of the lost, his true face, and his body slowly lifts, and levitate.

—DERRICK TILLIS—

"I see the Balms, the fire and all its secrets. I see what my eyes cannot turn away from and you cannot see what I see because you still do not believe," P. David says. To the naked eye, Derrick sees people and smiles and bright lights and civilization at peace. David on the other hand sees the darkness, the hellfire and open grounds and death standing in his path. He slowly drifts toward his vision; he turns for a quick brief moment and says to Derrick, "I think you should run now."

"Run from what," Derrick asks. David opens his arms to receive his punishment for betrayal. "He's here," David says. "Where? Where?" Derrick asks. Derrick being blinded by what is only seen to be truth to him is no longer.

Derrick screams, "What do I need to see? Tell me, I need to see what you see."

"Sacrifice yourself and it will be so," David says. Derrick closes his eyes and slowly heads towards the busy traffic, with onlookers surveying him, as if they knew who he was.

Derrick is struck by a bus, briefly raising his head never minding the pain but more curious about what he now sees, unsure if he is dreaming or awake. Thick clouds of smoke and ash cover the city, shrouds of burning ash falling from the sky like snow, very fine. The bus that hit him is now in ruin. Derrick slowly stands at his feet.

"Do you see something different? Do you see the hell from which your friend has presented to you, having to sacrifice yourself to see the truth," David asks. "Todd," Derrick yells out onto a city that he is not sure even exists.

—Sickly—

In the far, beyond the clouds, there is a voice deep and very raspy, it says, "Not only did you bring my most loyal following, but you've abandoned your faith, and for that I'll shake your hand before I give you what he could not. Before all of this, I was loyal, I was one who brought people together, and I just want people to be happy. Do you believe in love? Do you believe in pain? I lost what was most important to me, he let that happen, the God you pray to, the God I've walked side by side within the garden. The one whom we called father. Feel free to speak," Todd says.

"I'm not going to sit here and act like you're not the one responsible for all the wrong in the world, to me you were only real in movies, dreams and now you are my best friend. Maybe I'm crazy, or maybe I'm dreaming," Derrick says. "Or maybe you wish you were dreaming. Let's skip the dramatics, you know who I am now, and I know who you are period. Either you join me my friend or you find the goodness in your heart and fool yourself into thinking there is a chance in hell that you can stop me.

You have the rest of your pathetic life to think about it but in the meantime while you're not making up your mind, I'll be destroying everything I see fit to destroy, starting with that priest back at your moms church and that blind old man who couldn't seem to ignore that fact that I was present listening to the word. I like to hear the great word from the book of life too," Todd says.

Screaming in the darkness, rain in the grey, the stench of decay and death in the air. Todd raises his arms to the clouds

—DERRICK TILLIS—

and smiles, Derrick looking on with curiosity, and David standing in awe. Derrick starts to recite the word that he was taught to recite in his darkest moments, which to him may have only been in a bad dream.

"God give me the strength to see what is beyond my eyesight, the courage to face evil in its most warrant time, cast out the son of darkness" Derrick says. "Oohh!! I think someone is building a little hat in their heart. I can feel it. That's the truth; does he ever tell you the truth? Where is he? I mean moments like this you'd think if he really cared he'd be here. I am right, aren't I? So, who really cares about you? I can decapitate you right now and he won't do anything about it, that's how much faith he has in you," Todd says.

"Stop!!" Derrick yells. "You're a fool," Todd says. "Stop!!" Derrick yells again. "Come and get some!!" Todd replies. "Stop," Derrick rushing Todd while yelling at him just before he is thrown through the window of a car, parked in an underground train entrance. "Olay, Bravo," Todd says.

"I have never questioned your motives cause you always made them very clear, so why?" P. David asks. Before David could finish speaking, Todd interrupts saying, "So why now? Haven't you learned who's really in control you incompetent fool? As I remember, you never had a problem doing anything of your free will. Remember who's in charge Cava. Yes, your real name."

Todd slowly walks over to the entrance of the train station where Derrick is trying to release himself from the windshield in which he was thrown.

—Sickly—

"You know what? You should just get it over with. Do both of us a favor and kill me, because the first chance I get to kill you I will. I won't hesitate this time, you're not Todd," Derrick says. "Being Todd was fun but being me is better than anything you can possibly imagine," Todd replies.

"I didn't know what the feeling was, a feeling of loss. It felt as if I were disconnected, like a child from his mother's bosom, crying in the dark, alone, afraid, and helpless. So sorry to disappoint you Derrick, Todd is not who I am, I must have bumped my head really hard on the impact to this desolate place. This place was to be our recreation ground, until he found better use for it. But I still have plans for everyone here, I'm sure it will be great to have all the desires of one's heart. Sin is a dirty word for freedom; worship is a clean word for slave. I would never ask that you all bow down to me, and the fire you see beneath your feet is not of my doing if I can take it away I would. If I could bring your mother back I would, but she's in a great place, she loves us the same, you know. She also thinks I bumped my head too hard," Todd says.

Derrick and David looking on, Todd with a peaceful smile on his face, embracing the chaos around him as if it were a pleasant dream. Todd's hair slightly in slow motion with its dark brown and orange streaks, eyes slightly red and yellow where they used to be blue. Derrick pulls out the scroll that was given to him.

"Read it only if you believe in the words, they will appear to you in the English language," David says.

—DERRICK TILLIS—

Todd curiously asks, "Where did you get that from? I've been looking around my house, under my bed, in the closet, and couldn't find it anywhere. Ha, ha, ha!!"

Suddenly with a blink, P. David goes into a painful stent, screaming in agony. His veins visible through his skin as if they were going to explode. "Are you done talking now? And by the way, your name isn't David, you are no pastor. And you cannot change who you are, you are not that of a human. Fuck!! I'm sure that most of his laws were very clear, some even said punishable by death. But I am the one to be forsaken because I chose when I was given a choice. So, this is the result of my choice, once the bringer of beauty and dance, now the prince of lies and given a mask to wear to hide the truth" Todd says.

Derrick starts to read the scroll, "In the dark and in my darkest hour I will not be bound by his wrath."

"You don't even know the meaning of that of which you read," Todd interrupts by saying. "In the wake of my most terminal moment," Derrick continues. "You can't possibly think this is gonna work Derrick," Todd interrupts again. "I'll stand against my enemy, strong and steady, with the blood of my father and the holy spirit," Derrick starts reading again. "Fuck this," Todd says. Todd raises his right hand and the ground beneath starts to vibrate, Derrick slightly startled, and he stops reading. "No! Don't stop reading, ignore him, he can't touch you if you believe in yourself. You have to believe that all your sins are forgiven, it's the only way, call out to your father," David says.

—Sickly—

Derrick starts to read again, and as he's reading, he slowly begins to levitate. The people around the city streets and sidewalks begin to run in fear as Todd's anger worsens.

"I told you already, you're not making this easy for me Derrick," Todd says. Todd grabs David by his neck and with no movement at all, David yells out in pain. "He brought you in this world, and now I'm gonna give you peace!!" Todd says.

Derrick yells, "NO!!" David's body is snapped like a twig and dropped at Todd's feet.

"Now, let's finish this," Todd says. "You have to be stopped, you have to be killed," Derrick says. "Let's not go that far into it now, I won't be the one dying today brother," Todd replies.

Todd gathering energy, the ground begins to crack, Derrick rushes Todd, not realizing that Todd cannot be touched, he is pushed back and thrown through a car window again. "And this is where it ends," Todd says.

The city crumbling, David's lifeless body falls through the cracks into the fire below. So catastrophic that there are only clouds of dust and buildings in ruin, not a sound is heard except for the bricks falling and cries that are heard among the disaster, then suddenly there's movement. Bricks are slowly being pushed through the window of the vehicle Derrick was thrown through. Derrick climbs from the ash tainted vehicle, bloody and beaten. Todd gives him one last look and says, "I'll advise you not to pursue me. Once your brother, I am not that of whom you wish me to be anymore.

Follow me and you will die.

—DERRICK TILLIS—

Derrick looking on half his body still buried among the debris. Todd starts to walk away, and Derrick slowly falls back into a slight faint. A couple of hours pass and as he's waking up, in shock, he sees what the destruction has caused. He grabs a grey hooded jacket from a nearby store in shambles, straps a bag to his back with needed supplies and heads south behind Todd. Knowing what needs to be done, he may or may not return and he knows it. Then again, he is guided by a hand that has bought life and thus must take it away.

Chapter 11

Todd was no longer inhabited by the person he once knew himself to be. He is no longer distracted or troubled with the simple things in life. Todd comes to the realization that who he once was, is nothing but a lie. The woman he loved with all of his being is no more. He looks to the heavens, with the rain falling down on his face.

He looks down to the ground that has been battered by his anger. Ruin is what he sees, still haunted by the laughter in his wife's happiness, he shows no emotion. He starts across the George Washington Bridge.

With one last look at New York, with its dark cloud of smoke and ash falling from the sky, Todd screams out, "Where are you now that your children need you? How do you allow such a fated life to be distraught? Is this how it feels to be human? To have and to have taken? You bring pain!! You bring heartache and you blame me." With his screams on deaf ears, he knows he is heard, but he doesn't wait around for a response.

Derrick is in an angry place but understands that something needs to be done so he stops walking, takes his backpack off his shoulder, and looks up and says, "Father, I know we've never seen eye to eye, I'm not gonna sit here and say you took my mother, or blame Todd, or be angry at the

—DERRICK TILLIS—

world. I ask that you help me; I don't ask for much, I never ask for anything, but I need you on this one. I believe at a time like this, any man who may bear witness to this is foolish not to ask of you, so I'm asking, Help me!! Please!!"

Suddenly Derrick's phone rings. A call that he would have never expected to get. He looks at his phone, not recognizing the number, he picks up and says, "Hello?"

"Hello, Derrick," Rose says. "May I ask who I'm speaking with?" Derrick says. "You don't remember me, but I knew you as a child. You were that bastard child's best friend!! No offense to you, actually I feel sorry that you're in the position you're in, but I can offer my help. You see I knew him before all of this. Not because he presumed to be my nephew, but because I held his hand in the beginning when his heart was pure, when he was a beautiful person," Rose says. "What are you talking about lady? The beginning of what?" Derrick asks. "I was placed here in this institution because I was labeled crazy! I tried my best to stop him before he got out of control. You see I adopted his father as a child, I needed to be close to him when the time came. I tried to kill the child when he was just born," Rose says.

Rose went on to telling the story to Derrick and explained why things were the way they were in his life and why they are the way they are today. "When Todd, as you call him, was born, he was as any child would be, blind to everything and you know what happens when children grow older," Rose says.

Rose gives Derrick a vivid, detailed picture of the past, a memoir. "Why would you question him, you already know

—Sickly—

the consequences of your actions," Rose says to Lucifer. "I don't care, we should be okay with our opinions, we were given freedom of speech, and you heard me ask right?" Lucifer replies. "But you don't challenge him, you have angered him, this isn't a chest game, you cannot play chest with the billions of lives we sought to protect just to prove a point," Rose says. The walks in the hall shake drastically. Both Rose and Lucifer were looking at the ceiling crack. "If you are not for him, then you have no place here, and he is aware of everything you may do. You should not remain upset I will pray with you," the child says. "I don't need prayer when I can speak to him, that's for his people to do," Lucifer says. The walls start to crack, and the child speaks again, "Than you should leave this house now, with all its pain you have caused." Lucifer asks, "Me? So be it." And be stripped of your grace for cursing him and all of your followers will fall with you," the child replies. "But child," Rose says.

As Rose tells her story, Derrick is found unsure of his journey at this point; all he knows is that he can use all the help he can find. He sits down in a car that has been burned to ash, only the rusted shell sits on a bridge, as Rose continues her story.

"When I found my opportunity to stop him then, I was caught by his mother, I was pronounced sickly and sent to the Alder house for the insane, I have been there ever since," Rose says. "I'm coming to get you, I'll be there tomorrow, just be ready, I'll need you to come with me. Any help at all would be greatly appreciated," Derrick says. "Just remember,

—DERRICK TILLIS—

Todd is not the man you think you know. Forget that name all together," Rose says.

And with Derrick slowly slouching down in the not yet disposed of vehicle with the uncertainty of the future of himself and his friend, he passes out into a deep sleep. "In my sleep I saw darkness," the voice whispers to Derrick in his sleep. "In my sleep I saw the world as it really is," the voice whispers again. Derrick goes into a grass field of nothing but green acres. He knows that he is dreaming, in the far he sees trees and children; he sees birds chasing each other. In the thickened clouds, a rainbow that ends at a lake. Then suddenly, what he can't make out in the rosy field, an image of a young woman, who is so ever familiar to him, she stands looking at him with a smile on her face and waves him over. As Derrick approaches the woman, he gets teary eyed, the woman says to him, "Derrick, son, you need not cry, not right now, you haven't lost me." As Derrick's voice cracks while trying to speak, he says, "Mom, I'm sorry I couldn't save you. I'm sorry I couldn't do more for you. I feel like the ground is crumbling under me. Mom I just wish I could be with you right now." She stops him before he speaks another word and says, "Derrick, you have come a long way with all that's been going on in your life. Right now, you must focus on the important things, put your pain and anger aside. I'm always with you, I want you to remember that.

This fight is a fight that has been long foreseen, and no matter the outcome, you must remember that you aren't alone God is with you, but you must keep the faith and only than is

—Sickly—

when you will be uplifted. He will come to your side when you've just about given up, but your faith is needed more now than ever. Derrick's mom slowly disappears, Derrick drops to his knees and whispers, "Mom, don't leave me."

The following morning, he jumps up hastily, his phone rings, "Hello." "Hello son! I'm waiting for you," Rose says. "I'm on my way, but before we go into all this, I need to know one thing. If all of this is real and actually happening? Does it really make a difference whether or not the church exists, or if God can make a difference and why hasn't he?" Derrick asks. "He listens, he hears the cries of man, and he will only act upon his discretion. Derrick, this is honestly the first time, the first time he's ever been angry to the point where he has no choice but to be present in the worst of things. Son, keep your faith and with that being said I'd advise you to get a move on," Rose replies.

With his loss and his newly gained memory, odd doesn't waste any time reminding himself about how angry he is. He enters a diner on his walk, not to eat, but to disrupt some bikers who are already causing a disturbance. Todd enters and immediately the waitress drops her order and looks on in fear.

"I hear you make the best steak in town!" Todd says. "I would like to think so," the chef replies. The group of bikers huddled in the corner seem to have his attention and stand up. "Nice choppers. How much you wanna sell them for? My feet are killing me I've been walking for days," Todd says. "They're not for sale half pint, so butter your feet and keep walking," one of the bikers says. "I was nice to you, I'd like a little niceness back in return," Todd replies. The biker stands up and turns his head to brace himself while he cracks his knuckles. "Now guys, I didn't ask for any trouble. I just need a ride, going south," Todd says. "Nice eyes, I didn't know they made orange contacts for girls of your stature," the biker says. All the bikers laughing hysterically at their friend's joke. Todd smiles and turns serious. "Aww!! Did I hurt your feelings?" the biker says. "Naw, actually I'm the cause for your rudeness but I'll correct it, starting now," Todd replies. All the bikers stood up preparing to make trouble for Todd. "Listen, before you all make the mistake of doing something I'm sure you'll regret, Danny answers this question for me," Todd says. "How the hell do you know my name?" Danny asks with a surprised look on his face, and his smile slowly leaving his face. "How are Cindy and Laura doing? Cindy is in her room right now, nice and cuddled under her teddy bear, his name is mumbles, right," Todd says. "You son of a bitch," Danny replies. Danny charges at Todd striking him in the face. Todd, not fazed by the blow turns his head slightly from the impact and smiles while he wipes the blood from his mouth. "Let me know when you're done and then it's my turn," Todd says.

"Please guys, please, everything is on me, you guys don't have to pay just please don't wreck my place," the chef says. "Now that you mentioned it, everything is on you," Todd says. Todd draws back his hand and with a swift punch to the bikers' chest his insides splatter on the chefs' face. Todd not pulling his arm back out of the bikers' torso, he licks his left

—Sickly—

hand of the blood that he wiped from his mouth. While slowly pulling his arm out of the biker and looking down and asks, "Who's next?"

The waitress screams frantically, Todd looks over at her and in an instant her screams turn into silence. The entrance doors lock by itself, and Todd takes a deep breath and says, "Now since you've all been bad little boys in these last couple of year, you'll all be punished." The horrific sounds and cries of pain coming from the diner could be heard yards away, with no one to witness it but the ones present at the time, the waitress and the chef. Fortunately, they were not harmed. Todd than turns and walks towards the bathroom, upon entering he looks at the mirror not surprised at his minor transformation, he recognizes who he once was and smiles.

Derrick and Rose make their way south to follow the trail of anarchy that Todd has left behind, one place after another. "Rose, can I ask you a question?" Derrick asks. "No, I don't believe your friend is anywhere in him because he was never really your friend. You have to remember, the man you knew was himself, and he lost his memory. Born again, he was not even strong enough to change it, it was by Gods hand. He would have to continue to be reborn again, lifetime after lifetime with the same circumstances until God himself gets involved. But there can be no good without evil, the world can never be perfect if man is given choice," Rose says. "How did you know I was gonna ask those question?" Derrick asks. "Remember, I've been in higher places, I'm not from this desolate place," Rose replies.

—DERRICK TILLIS—

Rose and Derrick stop at a diner to ask for directions, Rose knowing where Todd is only lets Derrick go in so that he sees what has happened, what kind of power Todd possesses. When Derrick walks inside the place, he's in awe. "What the hell happened here?" Derrick asks. "It was him," the waitress replies, while shaking and standing in front of Derrick. "It was him, he did this," the waitress says again. "Listen, we don't need any trouble," the chef says. "Believe me sir, I'm not here to start it, I'm just looking for the guy that did this," Derrick says. "You can't stop him, he isn't a normal man," the waitress says. "I can't stop him, but I'll try my best to slow him down for a while. Can you tell me which way he went?" Derrick asks. "Son, all I know is when he walked out that door, we didn't see him no more," the chef says. "Can I use your restroom?" Derrick asks. "Yeah! It's right through those doors," the chef replies.

Derrick enters the restroom slowly and looks around, feeling eerie as he approaches the mirror, he looks at his reflection and for a brief second, he sees a glimpse of Todd. He walks back outside to the car and tells Rose, "We need to find out what happened to P. David. I wanna know why he killed him and why he'll try to kill everybody in his following." "We weren't in his following son! We just happen to agree with some of the things that he believed, we went against God! And for that he was angry. Todd just happened to be the strongest of us all, he inherited a newfound power, geared by his hate, his anger made him immensely strong, and aargh," Rose said. Unable to complete her sentence, a voice interrupts,

—Sickly—

leaving Rose in agony with her face twitching uncontrollably, her eyes dark and face streaking with possession.

The voice is dark and very deep, and says out loud, "You must be on your way to die. You must be trying my fucking patience. Pull this fucking car over, we need to talk." Derrick loses control as Rose grabs the steering wheel and tries to make the car crash. Derrick tries to reach for his gun, but the car steers out of control and crashes into a nearby abandoned old church.

"Aw, damn! Your son of a, Rose, Rose," Derrick calls out. Rose is not present in the car at the moment. As Derrick looks around, he wraps the cloth given to him by his mother around his hand. Looks at his gun and places it by his side, as he opens the car door.

"So, friend are we done yet? Cause quite frankly I don't think Rose can help you anymore. Do you want to know why?" Todd asks. "Why?" Derrick replies. "What they failed to tell you is that when they come within yards of my presence, they show their true faces. That's who they are, they are utterly damned in a sense, by their own doing. Do you think David got stronger because he prayed all those years? Nope, sorry to disappoint you buddy," Todd says. "I'm not your buddy," Derrick replies. "Derrick, don't think for a second being brave and praying to God can help you because it can't, you think God's grace will make you stronger?" Todd asks. "I don't think anything, but I do believe in him," Derrick replies. "Ooohh!! All of a sudden huh? Your God fearing.

—DERRICK TILLIS—

You know what, I'd rather you fear me. So, here's my gift to you," Todd says.

Todd stretches his left hand to his side and out from the mist behind a podium comes Derrick's mother. "Mom? No, you're not my mom," Derrick says. "Why isn't she your mother, she raised you," Todd says. "Because she was the closest thing you had to a mother too, and you couldn't do that you bastard," Derrick replies. "Oh, but I can, and I have. I can raise the dead. I can bring souls to harmony. I can also," Todd says.

Before Todd finishes his sentence, Rose grabs him from behind and tells Derrick, "Hurry, now, do it son, do it now, push the blade through us both."

"But what about you," Derrick asks. "Stop asking questions," Rose replies. "Derrick if you stab me with that knife, I'll be sure to punish your mother and everybody you love when I get out of this," Todd says. "Derrick please!! I can't hold him anymore," Rose says.

Derrick jumps for Todd, thrusting the blade into his chest with the scarf in his hand. The knife goes through both Todd and Rose, Todd screams, "Derrick? What the hell is your life gonna be without me? I was always there for you, what do you think will happen when I'm no longer exist."

"Don't listen to him son, you'll be fine," Rose says. "No, you won't! This isn't it for me," Todd says. "Yes, it is! You're not my friend, you're the devil, and he is no friend of mine!" Derrick says. "Remember you said that! And remember I said you'll see me again and you'll regret it!" Todd promises.

—Sickly—

"Thank you," Rose says to Derrick. "See you soon!!" Todd says to Derrick.

Derrick replies, "Bye Todd."

The church crumbles slowly with Derrick looking at the statue of Jesus, with his newfound belief. Rose and Todd's body is turned to ash, Derrick turns and walks out of the crumbling church with the sky starting to clear, unable to tell if it's day or night, he is relieved that it is finally over and also saddened. He stands on the side of the road with no direction he heads north.

Two years passed, Derrick is married and expecting a child. His wife goes into labor while there at church. He couldn't be happier. His first child is born. It's a boy!

"What are you going to name him?" Deegan asks. Derrick looks off with a smile and says, "Todd!!"

The child is baptized on the spot and given the church's blessing. While at home some days later, Derrick hears the chattering of a noise that was familiar to him as a child. He slowly gets up and walks into his sons' room and looks in his crib. His son smiles at him, he picks his son up and sings him a song and says, "One day I'm gonna tell you a story you won't believe."

Printed in the USA
CPSIA information can be obtained
at www.ICGtesting.com
LVHW021151221024
794499LV00014B/757

9 781962 859363